MIRAMAR

MIRAMAR

NAGUIB MAHFOUZ

Translated by
Fatma Moussa Mahmoud
Edited and revised by
Maged el Kommos
John Rodenbeck
Notes by
Omar el Qudsy

Introduction by
JOHN FOWLES

Published in Egypt by
The American University in Cairo Press
113 Sharia Kasr el Aini, Cairo, Egypt

Published in Great Britain by
Heinemann Educational Books Ltd.

First published in Arabic in 1967. Protected under the Berne
Convention. This English translation first published in 1978.
Copyright © 1978 The American University in Cairo Press.
Introduction © 1978 J. R. Fowles Ltd.
Notes © 1978 Omar el Qudsy

THE AMERICAN UNIVERSITY
IN CAIRO PRESS

Dar el Kutub No.
ISBN 977 424 000 8

Published in Egypt by
The American University in Cairo Press
113 Sharia Kasr el Aini, Cairo, Egypt
Published in Great Britain by·
Heinemann Educational Books Ltd

First published in Arabic 1967. Protected under the Berne
Convention. This English translation first published 1978.

Dar el Kutub No. 3052/85
ISBN 977 424 091 X

CONTENTS

INTRODUCTION   vii

1   AMER WAGDI   1

2   HOSNI ALLAM   38

3   MANSOUR BAHY   63

4   SARHAN EL-BEHEIRY   94

5   AMER WAGDI   124

NOTES   133

INTRODUCTION

Open cities are the mothers of open societies, and their existence is especially essential to literature—which is why, I suppose, we cherish our illusions about them, and forgive them so many of their sins. In the case of Alexandria, that prototype cosmopolis and melter of antitheses, we can hardly be blamed. *Antony and Cleopatra*, Cavafy, E. M. Forster, Lawrence Durrell ... there is a formidably distinguished list of foreign celebrants and from them we have taken an indelible image of the place. It is languorous, subtle, perverse, eternally *fin de siècle*; failure haunts it, yet a failure of such richness that it is a kind of victory. What we have conspicuously lacked, in this comfortable pigeon-holing, is a view from the inside, from modern Egypt herself. The one we are now granted may come as something of a shock to those who still see Alexandria through European eyes. Only the sense of failure remains ... and perhaps not least in the announcement of the death of the old city of our communal literary dream.

Though Naguib Mahfouz—now in his sixties—is his country's most distinguished novelist, with a formidable body of work behind him, it would be idle to pretend his name is familiar in the West. I am very sure it is not because he is not worth reading; but nor is it quite a case of mere insularity on our side. Cairo may be only a few hours' flight from London or Paris, but the cultural journey is much more complex and hazardous. Of all the world's considerable contemporary literature, that in Arabic must be easily the least known, which is one very good reason why the Arab mind remains something of a mystery to Westerners—and the more mysterious as it becomes more urban and sophisticated. In one way it is a misfortune that so many great English writers, such as Doughty and T. E. Lawrence, have concentrated on the Bedouin side of the story; very few of us have any clear picture at all of how twentieth century educated Islam lives, feels and thinks.

One obvious hurdle is the Arabic language itself. With its sharp distinction between spoken and literary forms, it is far from easy to translate into a pragmatic, almost purely vernacular language like English—with all its own time-honoured notions of the 'right' style and method in fiction. The differences among the spoken dialects of Arabic are much greater than among those in English; yet an Algerian and an Iraqi writer, because of the literary *lingua franca,* have no difficulty in reading each other's work. This much wider potential readership helps explain why serious writers in Arabic have resisted all attempts to evolve a demotic written form; but in addition the 'vulgar' forms of Arabic are principally languages of transaction, lacking the finesse and richness a novelist requires of his basic clay; and there are in any case purely technical problems, due to the nature of cursive script, in notating the vernacular. That does not mean a modern Arab writer cannot employ colloquial usages in certain areas. A translator has to allow for that—and then jump to the other historical extreme with all the echoes of *al 'arabiyyat al fusha,* the classical form fundamentally derived—despite a greatly enriched vocabulary—from the language of the Koran and the eighth century founding fathers of Arabic philology, al-Khalil and Sibawaih. These resonances are obviously nearly impossible to render in another tongue without descending to fustian and the mock-biblical.

Then stylistically Arabic has an odd conjunction of paucity of rhetorical device but great subtlety of syntax and grammar. A translator into English is faced with the constant problem of staying true to his text on the one hand and making some accommodation to English stylistic conventions on the other. To take two small examples, both ellipsis and repetition of words are favourite devices in Arabic ... and in general the very reverse in English. Perhaps the problem is best grasped by analogy with other arts; by recalling the difficulty of transcribing Arabic music, or of 'translating' the visual ellipsis and repetition characteristic of Islamic decorative technique into a European pictorial style.

This linguistic Iron Curtain has kept us miserably short of first-hand information about the very considerable changes that Egypt has undergone in this century; and that alone, quite apart from the novel's intrinsic merits, makes the publication of *Miramar* in English a most welcome thing. Though the book is set in Alexandria, it is essentially about Egypt itself and the normal conflicts—both public and personal—that have arisen during the successive revolutions of these last sixty years.

It is not for nothing that the better educated male characters in the story all revolve around the shrewd-naïve figure of the peasant-girl, Zohra. The fellaheen (from *falaha*, to till) are the heart of Egypt, and the heart of all its problems of social progress and national identity. Their age-old exploitation haunts every Egyptian conscience, just as their frequently mulish adherence to tradition is the despair of every Egyptian liberal—though it must be added that very little in the last five millennia has shown the fellaheen to be wrong in suspecting the motives of would-be world-changers descending on the Nile Valley. Their character was once described to me thus: 'Among the women the sole interest is sex, which is related to food and money; among the men the major interest is money, which is related to sex and food. Their lives are brutal; they live on an eternal frontier, where each year makes its own tradition, and strength is all that counts, so far beyond the reach of what we regard as civilization as to seem surreal, though we have all met their tough sweetness before, in the Russian novelists.'

That is clearly not quite the case with the heroine of *Miramar*. It is precisely her determination to emancipate herself that the men about her admire . . . or resent; and why they are perhaps best defined by their varying reactions to her, since she stands for Egypt itself. To Western readers the miseries of her situation may seem exaggerated, a shade 'Victorian' and melodramatic. I can say only that the peasant nursemaid in the house where I stayed in Cairo in 1972 had had very closely similar experiences to those of Zohra. She too was trying to educate herself, against intense family opposition—and in spite of the fact that they appropriated all her wages for their own upkeep. Only a month before I met her she had been publicly beaten in the street by her brother for refusing an old man her father had ordered her to marry for flagrant reasons of self-profit. Wahiba knew just enough English to have the story of my novel *The French Lieutenant's Woman* explained to her; and I count it as one of the most touching compliments I have ever been paid that this unhappy and courageous girl exclaimed, when she had understood the main theme, 'Oh it is my story, it is me.'

*　　*　　*

The symbolic overtones of this kind of exploitation, so skilfully used by Naguib Mahfouz, do not need elaborating. But a brief reminder (more fully amplified in the notes) must be given of the political and historical background to *Miramar*.

The driving spirit behind modern Egyptian nationalism was Sa'ad Zaghloul (1860–1927). His long opposition to both the Sultanate and the British Protectorate led eventually to his being deported to Malta in 1919, along with his leading supporters. The whole of Egypt rose in protest, and the exiles were finally allowed to send a *wafd*, or delegation, to the Versailles Peace Conference. Though they failed there, containing Wafdist agitation forced the Milner Commission to recommend termination of the Protectorate (though not a British 'presence', which lasted until 1954) in 1922. The first elections in 1924 gave the Wafd Party, which on this occasion had massive support from otherwise very disparate sections of society, a huge majority. Sa'ad Zaghloul became prime minister.

The history of the next three decades was one of continual political seesawing, with the much-needed internal social and economic reforms largely sacrificed to the land-owning interest, the enduring problem of Anglo-Egyptian relations, and party squabbles. The once solid Wafd Party itself split into factions. The 1952 arson and riots in Cairo helped bring about the *coup d'état* of July 23, carried out by a military junta headed (or more accurately, figureheaded) by General Mohammed Neguib. Both the monarchy and parliamentary government were abolished. Neguib gave way in 1954 to Colonel Nasser, who initiated the famous programme of social, educational and land reform—the Revolution, whose consequences are to be seen on every page of *Miramar*. The Revolution is now regarded in Egypt as an almost total failure; but then so was the French Revolution in France, at the same remove.

It must be remembered that politically the novel (published in 1967) is already dealing with past history. In the last decade Egypt has become far less of a socialist country than it appears in the pages that follow. Effective power now resides with a new urban bourgeoisie—the 'New Class', of whom President Sadat himself is an example. Statistically the top twentieth of the nation, this class had been quick to exploit, in a thoroughly capitalist way, the inherent weaknesses of Nasserist socialism—the population explosion, the growth of consumer demand, the switch from a shortlived national to a much deeper-rooted personal aspiration.

According to a recent report in *Time*, there are now as many millionaires in Egypt as during King Farouk's reign.

Appearing just before the disastrous 1967 war with Israel, the novel was a courageous anticipation of a subsequent 'loosening of tongues' or release of steam after the thirteen years of tight control of the press and the arts practised by the Nasser regime. Mahfouz had already, in 1959, incurred the wrath of El-Azhar University, the bastion of Moslem traditionalism, with a religious and social allegory *Awlad haratina*, or The Young Men In Our Alley, in which one of the characters is God, and Moses, Jesus and Mohammed also appear. Despite his very considerable prestige ('approaching pharaohdom' in the tart phrase of one Cairo critic), he was obliged to publish in the Lebanon. In 1967 *Miramar*, with its far from kind view of the 'centres of power' (*scilicet* the Arab Socialist Union), reflected perfectly the feelings many Egyptian intellectuals had held in private towards the political excesses and mistakes of the past decade.

However, Mahfouz is most certainly not some Egyptian equivalent of an English Tory. His disillusionment was far less with specific policies and theories of the Egyptian left than with the moral failure (best represented in his novel by the figure of Sarhan) of the Revolution in practice. What haunts his novel, indeed, is something deeper than disillusion: despair at the eternal and cruel dilemma of his country. Western concepts like 'social equality' and 'freedom of the individual' have little meaning in Egypt, where the legal system is exiguous and the judiciary have no power over the executive. In any case, the country allows exceptional social mobility. It has to, when almost everyone is engaged in a no-holds-barred struggle for personal economic survival. Mahfouz's view is therefore more akin to the stoical, pessimistic side of humanism, both European and Islamic. History and geography are the fundamental villains; or the nature of things. We are perhaps not too far removed from the spirit of the most famous of Cavafy's poems.

> *Now what's going to happen to us without barbarians?*
> *Those people were a kind of solution.*

Two classes suffered, the one economically, the other morally, during the attempt to found a Moslem socialism—the rich and the ambitious. The first, the hereditary landlords, are represented in the novel by Tolba Bey and Hosni Allam, the blind reaction of one generation turned into the feckless nihilism of the next; and the second class, the ambitious, by Sarhan and Mansour—the one sunk in an amoral hypocrisy, a blend of Tartuffe and Uriah Heep, the other retreated into a sort of narcissistic no-man's land. This latter pair may, I think, be seen as inevitable victims of a world locked in battle over the frontier between social good and personal survival.

An excellent new study of Egypt's economic problems* makes it clear why the country feels this conflict with peculiar acuteness. Egypt is poor in natural resources and consequently short of white-collar jobs, a situation not helped by the great expansion, admirable in itself, in educational facilities since 1954. On top of that, population growth has been steadily accelerating (it now stands at some 2.5% *per annum*) and combines politically 'difficult' features of high density and youthful composition. Almost all major Egyptian institutions in both private and public sectors are painfully overstaffed, with lamentable effects on managerial efficiency and productivity. Qualifications mean very little; and influence, very nearly all, which explains the importance given to the marriage theme in *Miramar*. All that really happened in the Revolution was that wealth and influence were redistributed among a new elite; the detritus of the old was despatched to the Pension Miramar.

It is against this background that the predicament of the three young men in *Miramar* should be read, and their egocentricity, their lostness, their duplicity, understood. But, of course, such victims of greater circumstance, torn between self-interest and self-contempt, exist everywhere today, both East and West; and although some of the outward signs of tension—the outbursts of inappropriate laughter, the sudden plunges into sincere respect and emotion—may be specifically Egyptian, the basic type is surely universal. If we set aside moral judgements, perhaps the most attractive of the younger men is the playboy, Hosni. At least he is going down in style. His strange and memorable slogan, *ferekeeko*, is explained in the notes; and again, in one form or another, some very similar word or phrase has crept into almost every language in recent years. Again the keynote is despair—young blood defeated by the irremediable faults of a very old world.

One other fickle element, quite literally element, in *Miramar* requires a brief comment: that is the weather. The repeatedly

---

* Robert Mabro, *The Egyptian Economy 1952–1972*, Oxford University Press (1974).

evoked clouds, storms and rain certainly reflect a society in painful evolution, but one may guess that they are also emblematic of the unpredictability of history, of forces beyond human control. Rain may suggest hope and fertility in the West, but we are in a grimmer, more fatalistic world here. So is it with the remnants of the old cosmopolitan Alexandria; Egypt is beyond help from that direction, too, now.

* * *

Naguib Mahfouz* was born in 1912, by nine years the youngest sibling of a lower middle-class family in Cairo, which meant that he was effectively brought up as an only child. He showed early promise in his own language, as also in history and the sciences. At eighteen he encountered Darwin, and this led to a severe crisis of faith. He entered the King Fuad I (now Cairo) University in 1930 as a student of philosophy. The lectures were then given in English and French and Mahfouz had difficulty in following them. To remedy this he translated James Baikie's *Ancient Egypt*.

On graduation in 1934 Mahfouz considered an academic career, but two years later he opted for writing, in spite of the poor financial rewards. His first three books received no payment at all, and gained him a nickname—*al Sabir*, or 'the patient one'. Like all Egyptian writers, he had to look elsewhere for a living. He began as a university secretary, and then between 1939 and 1954 was employed in the Ministry of Religious Affairs. His subsequent work in the civil service was to do with the arts, most latterly as Consultant for Cinema Affairs to the Ministry of Culture. He retired from this post in 1972.

He did not develop an interest in foreign literature before his student days. One very strong influence then was certainly that of the British social-realist novelists of the beginning of the century: Galsworthy, Wells and Arnold Bennett. He also read the Victorian novelists, though curiously the one writer, Dickens, who might appear to have sparked Mahfouz's own brilliant descriptions of the Cairo poor, seems never to have impressed him—indeed, he once confessed he had never managed to finish a Dickens story.

---

* I owe this brief account to a monograph by Marsden Jones and Hamdi Sakkut: *Najib Mahfuz, a bio-bibliographical study*. I should also like to add here my thanks to Dr. John Rodenbeck of the American University in Cairo for much general help and advice throughout this introduction.

xiii

His literary interests broadened very considerably over the years. In French he admires Balzac, Proust, Sartre and (no surprise to anyone who reads the second section of *Miramar*) Camus. Joyce, Huxley, Orwell, Faulkner and Hemingway are among his preferred writers in English. His knowledge of ancient Arabic literature is slight, and among his contemporaries in modern Arabic literature, the only clear influence is from Tawfiq al-Hakim.

His work can be broadly divided into three periods. He began with three historical (the so-called 'pharaonic') novels, but then wrote a series on social themes, the masterpiece of which was the *Trilogy* (completed in 1957). This huge and partly autobiographical work revealed the struggles and convolutions of Egyptian society with a Balzacian breadth and degree of technical innovation unparalleled in any other writer of his time. Some critics have complained of over-richness and plot proliferation, but the achievement was considerable.

His second period, beginning in 1959, forsook social realism for metaphysical allegory, or man in society for man in time, and showed a much increased use of symbolism and the stream-of-consciousness technique, sometimes resulting in a language nearer to poetry than to prose. The third period, dating from *Miramar* in 1967, shows a synthesis of these two rather different previous stages in his growth. Mahfouz has also published seven collections of short stories—there have been four since 1969—whose themes and styles echo the development in his novels. In general the tendency on this side of his writing has been to abandon conventional realism.

Mahfouz is not without his critics in his own country, as I have already suggested. He may be something of a literary pharaoh; but at least he appears to be a refreshingly modest one. Philip Stewart records the following of a conversation with him.

'Mahfouz's reticence comes from a deep-seated humility which can be illustrated by his view of his own work. He is glad that his books are read and agrees that he is amongst Egypt's leading authors; but, when asked how he would rate his own books in relation to European literature, he said they were "probably, like the rest of modern Arabic literature, fourth or fifth rate". He suggested tentatively Shakespeare, James Joyce and Tolstoy as examples of first-rate writing, and Wells, Dickens, Thackeray, Shaw, Galsworthy, Huxley and D. H. Lawrence as second or third-rate European writers. Asked for examples of even lesser European writers, he said he had never read any and was not interested to do so, adding that he did not suppose many Europeans would be interested in modern Arabic literature as it has produced only such writing. He supposes that the reason for this is that literature is formed by its social context and by the attitudes of its readers, and that, since Egypt is still undergoing the industrial and social revolution which Europe passed through a hundred and fifty years ago, Arabic literature must use the technique and subject-matter of the nineteenth century. While there is nothing startling about this view, it is remarkable that it should be held by Egypt's best-selling novelist.'

* * *

Clearly it is not easy for Westerners to place a writer so adamantly self-disparaging (even if one suspects Koranic precept plays a part in the judgement), and the greater part of whose work remains untranslated and therefore unknown. But I think few will disagree that we are with *Miramar* in the hands of a considerable novelist, and one who knows his country's complex problems, and complex soul, profoundly. Work of this quality also explains why Egypt was long seen by other Arabs as the literary leader of their world.

Like all novels worth their salt, *Miramar* allows us the rare privilege of entering a national psychology, in a way that a thousand journalistic articles or television documentaries could not achieve; and perhaps more importantly, beyond that, we can encounter in it a racial temperament that has been widely misunderstood in the West. The sometimes bizarre emotional mobility of the younger characters, their disorientation, their sensibility, their strikingly Romantic (shades of Chateaubriand) addiction to despair and *Weltschmerz* ... these things may seem rather remote from our general picture of the Egyptian character, at any rate as formed by our image of their more recent political leaders. But this is an active, and unimpeachably witnessed, view of what we too often see as a passive—or impassive—culture.

If it cannot dispel every illusion or ignorance we hold about Egypt, it represents a very considerable first step. I sincerely hope that the reader will share the pleasure and interest I have got from this very revealing, and very human, novel.

JOHN FOWLES

1. AMER WAGDI

Alexandria. At last. Alexandria, Lady of the Dew.[1] Bloom of white nimbus. Bosom of radiance, wet with sky-water. Core of nostalgia steeped in honey and tears.

The massive old building confronts me once again. How could I fail to recognize it? I have always known it. And yet it regards me as if we had shared no past. Walls paintless from the damp, it commands and dominates the tongue of land, planted with palms and leafy acacias, that protrudes out into the Mediterranean to a point where in season you can hear shotguns cracking incessantly.[2]

My poor stooped body cannot stand up to the potent young breeze out here. Not any more.

Mariana, my dear Mariana, let us hope you're still where we could always find you. You must be. There's not much time left; the world is changing fast and my weak eyes under their thinning white brows can no longer comprehend what they see.

Alexandria, I am here.

On the fourth floor I ring the bell of the flat. The little judas opens, showing Mariana's face. Much changed, my dear! It's dark on the landing; she does not recognize me. Her white face and golden hair gleam in the light from a window open somewhere behind her.

'Pension Miramar?'

'Yes, monsieur?'

'Do you have any vacant rooms?'

The door opens. The bronze statue of the Madonna receives me. In the air of the place is a kind of fragrance that has haunted me.

We stand looking at each other. She is tall and slim, with her golden hair, and seems to be in good health, though her shoulders are a little bowed and the hair is obviously dyed. Veins show through the skin of her hands and forearms; there are tell-tale wrinkles at the corners of her mouth. You must be sixty-five at least, my dear. But there is still something of the old glamour left. I wonder if you'll remember me.

She looks me over. At first she examines me; then the blue eyes blink. Ah, you remember! And my self comes back to me.

'Oh! It's you.'

'Madame.'

We shake hands warmly— 'Goodness me! Amer Bey! Monsieur Amer!'—and she laughs out loud with emotion (*the long feminine laugh of the fishwives of Anfushi!*)[3] throwing all formality to the winds. Together we sit down on the ebony settee beneath the Madonna, our reflections gleaming on the front of a glassed bookcase that has always stood in this hall, if only as an ornament. I look round.

'The place hasn't changed a bit.'

'Oh but it has,' she protests. 'It's been redecorated a number of times. And there are many new things. The chandelier. The screen. And the radio.'

'I'm so glad to have found you here, Mariana. Thank Heaven you're in good health.'

'And so are you. Monsieur Amer—touch wood.'

'I'm not at all well. I'm suffering from colitis and prostate trouble. But God be thanked all the same!'

'Why have you come here now? The season's over.'

'I've come to stay. How long is it since I saw you last?'

'Since . . . since . . . did you say "to stay"?'

'Yes, my dear. I can't have seen you for some twenty years.'

'It's true. You never turned up once during all that time.'

'I was busy.'

'I bet you came to Alexandria often enough.'

'Sometimes. But I was too busy. You know what a journalist's life is like.'

'I also know what men are like.'

'My dear Mariana, *you* are Alexandria to me.'

'You're married, of course.'

'No. Not yet.'

'And when will you marry, monsieur?' she asks teasingly.

'No wife, no family. And I've retired.' I reply somewhat irritably. 'I'm finished.' She encourages me to go on with a wave of her hand. 'I felt the call of my birthplace. Alexandria. And since I've no relations I've turned to the only friend the world has left me.'

2

'It's nice to find a friend in such loneliness.'

'Do you remember the good old days?'

'It's all gone,' she says wistfully.

'But we have to go on living,' I murmur.

When we start discussing the rent, however, she can still drive as hard a bargain as ever. The Pension is all she has; she has had to take in winter guests, even if they are those awful students; and to get them she is forced to depend on middlemen and waiters in the hotels. She says it all with the sadness of humbled pride; and she puts me in number six, away from the sea front on the far side, at a reasonable rent, though I can retain my room in the summer only if I pay at the special summer rate for holiday makers.

We settle everything in a few minutes, including the obligatory breakfast. She proves as good a businesswoman as ever, notwithstanding sweet memories and all that. When I tell her I've left my luggage at the station, she laughs.

'You were not so sure you'd find Mariana. Now you'll stay here with me forever.'

I look at my hand and think of the mummies in the Egyptian Museum.

*　　*　　*

My room is pleasant enough, quite as good as any of the seaward rooms I used to occupy in the past. I have all the furniture I need. Comfortable, old-fashioned chairs. But there is no place for the books; I'd better leave them in the box and take out only a few at a time. The light here is not very good, a sort of constant twilight. My window opens on to a big air-shaft and the service stairs are so close that I can hear alley-cats chasing up and down and cooks and chambermaids carrying on their affairs.

I make the round of all the rooms where I used to stay in summer; the pink, the violet and the blue, all vacant now. There was a time when I stayed in each a summer or more, and though the old mirrors, the rich carpets, the silver lamps and the cut glass chandeliers are gone, a certain faded elegance lingers still on the papered walls and in the high ceilings, which are adorned with cherubs.

Mariana sighs and I see her false teeth.

'Mine was a very select *pension*.'

' "Glory be to Him who remaineth".'

'These days, my guests in winter are mostly students. And in summer I take just anybody.

* * *

'*Amer Bey, will you please put in a good word for me?*'
'Your Excellency,' I said to the Pasha[4], 'the man is not very efficient, but he lost his son in the Cause and should be nominated for the seat.'
He backed my proposal. God rest his soul. My great Master. He loved me and read everything I wrote with the keenest interest.
'You,' he said to me once, 'are the Nation's throbbing cur.'
He said *cur* for *core*, God rest his soul, and it became a standing joke. A few old colleagues from the National Party heard the story and they'd always greet me with 'Hello, you cur!' Those were the days—the glory of working for the Cause, independence, the Nation! Amer Wagdi was someone indeed—full of favours for friends, but a man to be feared and avoided by enemies.
In my room I reminisce, read, or sleep. In the hall I can talk to Mariana or listen to the radio. If I need further entertainment there is the Miramar Café downstairs. It is not likely that I should see anyone I know, even in the Trianon.[5] All my friends are gone. The good old days are over.
Alexandria, I know you in winter: you empty your streets and your squares at sunset, leaving them to solitude, wind and rain, while your inner rooms are filled with chatter and warmth.

* * *

' " . . . that old man shrouding his mummified form in a black suit that dates from the Flood." None of your long-winded rhetoric, please!' said that nonentity of an editor, so typical of these days. 'Give us something a jet-age traveller can read.'
A jet-age traveller. What would you know, you fat moronic puppet? Writing is for men who can think and feel, not mindless sensation-seekers out of nightclubs and bars. But these are bad times. We are condemned to work with upstarts, clowns who no doubt got their training in a circus and then turned to journalism as the appropriate place to display their tricks.

* * *

4

I sit in an armchair wearing my dressing-gown. Mariana reclines on the ebony settee beneath the statue of the Madonna. Dance music is being played on the European Programme. I would rather listen to something different, but I hate to disturb her. She is completely absorbed in the music, just as she always used to be, nodding her head to its beat.

'We've always been friends, Mariana.'

'Yes, always.'

'But we never made love, not once.'

'You went in for your plump countrywomen. Don't deny it.'

'Except for that one incident. Do you remember?'

'Yes, you brought home a Frenchwoman and I insisted that you sign the register as Monsieur and Madame Amer.'

'I was discouraged by the multitude of your aristocratic admirers.'

She beams with pleasure. Mariana, let's hope I may be the first of us two to go; no more shifting quarters. There you are, a living proof that the past was no illusion, even from the days of my great Master down to the present moment.

'*My dear sir, I'd like to say goodbye.*' *He looked at me, as usual not bothering to disguise his impatience.* '*At my age, I think I should retire.*'

'*We shall certainly miss you,*' *he answered with ill-concealed relief,* '*but I hope you'll have a good time.*'

That was all. A page of the newspaper's history turned without a word of goodbye, a farewell party, or even a jet-age snippet at the bottom of a page. Nothing. The buggers! A man has no value to them at all unless he plays football or something.

As she sits there under the statue of the Madonna, I look at her and say, 'Helen in her prime would not have looked as marvellous!'

She laughs. 'Before you arrived, I used to sit here all alone waiting for someone, anyone I knew, to come through the door, I was always in dread of ... of getting one of my kidney attacks.'

'I'm sorry. But where are your people?'

'They've gone, every one of them.' She purses her lips, showing her wrinkles. 'I couldn't leave—where should I go? I was born here. I've never even seen Athens. And after all, who'd want to nationalize a little *pension* like this?'

'*Let us be true to our word and devoted to our work and may love, not law, control man's dealings with man.*' *Look at us now. It*

5

was a kindness of God to give you death when he did—with a couple of statues as your memorial.

'Egypt's your home. And there's no place like Alexandria.'

The wind plays outside. The darkness steals up quietly. She rises, switches on two bulbs of the chandelier and returns to her seat.

'I was a lady,' she says, 'A lady in the full sense of the word.'

'You're still a lady, Mariana.'

'Do you still drink the way you used to?'

'Just one drink at dinner. I eat very little. That's why I can still move around.'

'Monsieur Amer, I don't know how you can say there's no place like Alexandria. It's all changed. The streets nowadays are infested with *canaille*.'

'My dear, it had to be claimed by its people.' I try to comfort her and she retorts sharply.

'But *we* created it.'

'And you, do you still drink the way you did in the old days?'

'No! Not a drop. I've got kidney trouble.'

'We should make two fine museum pieces. But promise me you won't go before I do.'

'Monsieur Amer, the first revolution killed my first husband. The second took my money and drove out my people. Why?'

'You've got enough, thank God. *We* are your people[6] now. This sort of thing is happening everywhere.'

'What a strange world.'

'Can't you tune the radio to the Arabic station?'

'No. Only for Umm Kulthum.'[7]

'As you wish, my dear.'

'Tell me, why do people hurt one another? And why do we grow old?'

I smile, not saying a word. I look around at the walls, which are inscribed with Mariana's history. There is the Captain's portrait, in full dress, heavy-whiskered—her first husband, probably her first and only love, killed in the Revolution of 1919.[8] On the other wall, above the bookcases, is the portrait of her old mother, a teacher. At the opposite end of the hall, beyond the screen, is her second husband, a rich grocer, 'The Caviare King', owner of the Ibrahimiya Palace. One day he went bankrupt and killed himself.

'When did you start this business of the Pension?'

'You mean, when was I forced to open a boarding-house? In 1925. A black year.'

6

'*Here I am, almost a prisoner in my house, and the hypocrites queue up to flatter the King.*'

'*All lies, your excellency.*'

'*I thought the Revolution had cured them of their weaknesses.*'

'*The true heart of the nation is on your side. Shall I read you tomorrow's editorial?*'

She sits there massaging her face with a piece of lemon.

'I was a lady, Monsieur Amer. Living the easy life and loving it. Lights, luxury, fine clothes and big parties. I would grace a salon with my presence. Like the sun.'

'I saw you then.'

'You saw me only as a landlady.'

'But you were still like the sun.'

'My guests did belong to the elite. But that has never consoled me for such a comedown.'

'You're still a lady. In every sense.'

She shakes her head. 'What happened to all your old friends in the Wafd?'

'What was fated to happen.'

'Why did you never marry, Monsieur Amer?'

'Sheer bad luck. I wish I had a family. And you as well!'

'Neither of my husbands could give me children.'

More than likely it was you who couldn't conceive. A pity, my dear. Isn't the whole purpose of our existence to bring children into the world?

That big house in Khan Gaafer, which slowly turned into a hotel: it looked like a little castle, it's old courtyard standing where a path now runs to Khan El-Khalili. The image of the place is engraved in my memory—the ancient houses around it, the old Club—and in my heart. *A memorial to the ecstasy of first love. Burning love. Broken. Frustrated.* The turban and the white beard and the cruel lips saying 'No'. Blindly, fanatically dealing the blow, killing love, whose power has been with us for a million years, since even before the birth of faith.

'Sir, may I ask for your daughter's hand?' Silence. Between us stood a cup of coffee, untouched. 'I am a journalist. I have a good income. My father was the keeper of the Mosque of Sidi Abu el-Abbas el-Morsy.'

'He was a pious man, God rest his soul,' he said, taking up his prayer beads. 'My son, you were one of us. You studied in al-Azhar[9] once. But don't let us forget that you were expelled.'

That old story, when would they forget it?

'Sir, that was a long time ago. They'd expel you for the least thing—for being young and full of spirit, for playing in an orchestra or just for asking innocent questions.'

'Wise men accused you of a terrible crime.'

'Who can judge a man's faith, when only God sees through our souls?'

'Those who take God's words for a guide.'

God damn it! Who can be sure of his faith? To His prophets God revealed himself once, but we need to see Him even more: when we consider our place in this enormous house we call the world, our heads begin to reel.

*   *   *

Beware of idleness. I had better try walking on sunny mornings. How pleasant to spend a warm day at the Palma or the Swan, even if you are all on your own in the midst of so many families; the father reading his paper, the mother sewing, the children playing around them. Someone should invent a machine that would hold conversations with lonely people, a robot to partner us at backgammon or tric-trac. Or we should be given a brand new pair of eyes, so we could watch the plants of the earth or the colours of the sky.

I have lived long and seen so many eventful changes. I have often thought of writing it all down, as did my old friend Ahmed Shafiq Pasha, but I've put it off for so long that my strength of purpose has evaporated. Too late now! my hand is too weak, my memory cloudy and nothing is left of the old intention but the sense of frustration. At this point I may commend to ashes my 'Azhar Memories', 'Conversations with the Great Musicians Sheikh Aly Mahmoud, Zakariya Ahmad, and Sayed Darwish', 'The People's Party: Its Pros and Cons', 'The Wafd and the Great Revolution'. Party differences, which eventually drove me into cold and meaningless neutrality. The Muslim Brethren, whom I did not like, the Communists, whom I did not understand. The July Revolution and what it meant, taking all previous political currents unto itself. My love life and Sharia Mohammad Aly.[10] My determined stand against marriage.

Yes, my memoirs would make a wonderful book—if they were ever written.

I have paid a nostalgic visit to the Atheneus, Pastoroudis and the Antoniadis and have sat for some time in the lobbies of the

Cecil and the Windsor,[11] the places where pashas and foreign politicians used to meet in the old days, the best places to pick up news. I saw no one I knew, only a few foreigners, Westerners and orientals, and made my way home with two silent prayers: may God help me back to the fold of His Faith . . . and may I die on my feet!

*　　*　　*

A lovely portrait, throbbing with youth and life: a young woman, her right knee on a chair, her left foot resting lightly on the floor, her wrists poised on the back of the chair, bending forward facing the camera and smiling with a proud sense of her own beauty, the extravagant décolletage of her old-fashioned dress showing a graceful neck and marble-white bosom.

Mariana sits in her black coat and navy blue scarf, waiting to leave for her appointment with the doctor.

'You said you lost your money because of the Revolution?'

She raises her pencilled eyebrows. 'Haven't you heard of the stock market crash?' She can see the questioning look in my eyes. 'That's when I lost all the money I'd made during the Second World War. And believe me, it was made out of courage. I stayed on in Alexandria, when everyone else had run off to Cairo and the country. I wasn't afraid of the German air raids. I painted the windowpanes blue and drew the curtains and let them dance by candlelight. You never saw anything like the generosity of His Britannic Majesty's officers!'

After she leaves I sit on my own, staring into the eyes of her first husband, who stares from his gilt frame back at me. I wonder who killed you, and how? How many of my generation did you kill before you came to your end? The generation that outdid all others in the extent of its sacrifice. Those were the days. So many fallen.

*　　*　　*

This foreign singing never stops. It is the worst trial of my solitary existence. Returning from her doctor's, Mariana has had a hot bath. Now she sits in the hall wrapped in a white bathrobe, her dyed hair done up and covered all over with dozens of white-metal curlers. She turns the sound of the radio down to a whisper in order to start her own broadcast.

'Monsieur Amer, you must have plenty of money.'

'Do you have any project in hand?' I ask cautiously.

'Not really, but at your age, and mine too—though there is such a big difference—our worst enemies are poverty and ill health.'

'I've always had enough for my needs and I hope to die with an easy mind.' I remain on my guard.

'I don't remember that you were ever a spendthrift.'

I laugh. 'I hope my savings may outlive me.'

She waves her hand carelessly. 'The doctor was very encouraging today. I promised him I'd throw off all my cares.'

'That's good.'

'So we must have some fun on New Year's Eve.'

'Yes. If our hearts can bear it.'

'Oh, those wonderful parties!' She wags her head, beaming with recollected pleasure. 'These old memories stir up the embers,' she says wistfully.

'You were loved by many great men.'

'I was truly in love only once.' She points to the Captain's portrait. 'He was killed by one of those students. Fancy my slaving for them now! This used to be the *pension* for quality. I had a cook working for me, his assistant, a waiter, a laundress and two other servants. Now it's a charwoman, once a week.'

'Many of the "quality" would envy you now.'

'Don't make fun of me, Monsieur Amer.'

I say hesitantly: 'They would. If they knew.'

Her face grows grave and I laugh to cheer her up.

*　　*　　*

The Beneficent
Hath made known the Koran.
He hath created man.
He hath taught him utterance.
The sun and the moon are made punctual.
The stars and the trees adore
And the sky He hath uplifted; and He hath set
the measure.

Sunk deep in the big chair, my feet resting on a cushion, I am reading the Sura of the Beneficent,[12] dear to my heart since my days at al-Azhar. Outside is a heavy downpour, the rain drumming loudly on the iron stairs in my air-shaft.

Everyone that is thereon will pass away,
There remaineth but the countenance of thy Lord of Might
and Glory.

I hear voices in the hall. Is it a guest or a new lodger? Mariana's tones are too warm for a stranger—it must be an old friend. I hear laughter, too, a hollow male voice. Who can it be?

It is early in the afternoon and it is still raining hard, the clouds decanting enough darkness into the room to make it seem like night. I reach to turn on a lamp but as I press the switch the shutters gleam with lightning and I hear rolling thunder.

O company of jinn and men, if ye have power to penetrate
all regions of the heavens and the earth, then penetrate them:
Ye will never penetrate them save with Our sanction.

He is thick-set, with pudgy cheeks, a double chin and blue eyes, in spite of his dark skin. Unmistakably an aristocrat, a silent, proud man. His hands move with calculated precision when he speaks. Madame introduces him in the evening as Tolba Bey Marzuq: 'He was Under-secretary of State for the Ministry of Mortmain Endowments[13] and a great landowner.'

I have no need of further introduction. I had known him well enough in my profession, from those years of political and party conflicts. He was one of the King's henchmen and naturally an enemy of the Wafd. I recall that his property had been put under sequestration a year ago, with all his resources confiscated, leaving only the usual allowance. Mariana is in her best mood. She speaks repeatedly of their old friendship. Her warmth is explained when she calls him her 'old flame'.

'I read a great deal, years ago, of what you used to write,' he remarks. I laugh pointedly and so does he. 'Yours was a good example of a fine pen serving a bad cause.' He laughs again, but I will not let myself be drawn into an argument.

'Tolba Bey is an old graduate of the Jesuit schools,' Madame says smugly. 'We shall listen together to the French songs on the radio.' She adds, opening her palms wide in welcome: 'He's come to stay.'

'That's nice.'

'He had a thousand feddans.[14] Money was nothing to him,' she says nostalgically. 'A mere plaything.'

'No more playing now.' He is obviously piqued.

'Where is your daughter, Tolba Bey?'

'In Kuwait. Her husband's in business.'

I'd heard that Tolba Bey had been under suspicion for some attempt to smuggle his money out of the country, but his explanation is simple .'I had to pay for a piece of momentary folly.'

'Was there an investigation?'

'They wanted my money,' he says contemptuously, 'that's all.'

Mariana scrutinized him thoughtfully. 'You've changed a great deal, Tolba Bey.'

'I had a stroke,' he says, smiling with the little mouth that is buried in his fat cheeks. 'Almost knocked me off. But I'm all right now. I can even drink whisky, in moderation.'

*   *   *

He dipped the bun in his tea, eating slowly, for he was obviously not used to his new set of teeth. We were alone at breakfast. A few days had brought us nearer to one another. The sense of companionship had got the better of the old political differences as well as the deeply rooted aversion of two opposed temperaments, though occasionally the buried differences would drift up to the surface, reawakening an ugly antagonism.

'Do you know what really caused all those misfortunes of ours?'

'What misfortunes?' I asked, taken by surprise.

'You old fox! You know perfectly well what I mean!' He raised his grey eyebrows. 'They've abolished your party's name and following, just as they've confiscated our money.'

'You've forgotten that I left the Wafd—and all party politics—after February Fourth.'[15]

'No matter. They have stricken the pride of all our generation.'

I had no inclination to argue. 'All right. And so?'

'One man is responsible for this,' he said deliberately, with a deep note of loathing. 'This chain tightening round our necks. And strangely enough, hardly anyone mentions him.'

'Who's that?'

'Saad Zaghloul.'[16]

It was so preposterous that I laughed in his face.

'But he is!' he retorted sharply. 'He started all these troubles. This class business. His impudence, his arguing the toss with the King and playing up to the masses was only the beginning. It was an evil seed he sowed. And now like a cancer it'll finish us, one and all.'

*   *   *

There were only a few visitors at the Palma. Tolba Marzuq sat staring at the sluggish Nile water running in the Mahmoudiya Canal.[17] I stretched out my legs and sat back in my chair, drinking in the pristine rays of the sun. We had left the windy sea-front for this quiet haven at the far end of the city. It was a pleasant spot among the dense foliage of flowers and trees, warm and sunny on fine days.

For all his aggressive bad temper, I could not help pitying him. To have to start a bitter new life after sixty! He envied his daughter the bliss of exile, and he had strange dreams. He had no patience whatever with any social theory that could justify his personal misfortune as an historical necessity: any attempt against his property was a breach of the laws of God and Nature.

'You know, I almost decided to leave the *pension* when I learned that you were there.'

'But why?'

'I chose the Miramar in the hope that apart from that foreign woman I'd have the place to myself.'

Why had he changed his mind then?

'It seemed to me that I'd never heard of anyone over eighty playing Judas.'

That amused me very much. Was there any reason to fear government agents?

'None, really. But I sometimes need to find consolation in just talking. And I can't live in the country.' He went on with rising anger. 'They've taken my house. And in Cairo the atmosphere is a constant humiliation. So I thought of my old mistress. I said to myself: 'She's lost her husband in one revolution—and her money in the other. We'll be a fit match for each other.'''

A little later, he congratulated me on my good health, in spite of my age, and tried to persuade me to go with him to a cinema or an indoor café. Suddenly he asked:

'Why has God stopped using his powers?' And when I did not understand. 'Why? Floods, catastrophic storms . . .'

'Do you think the Flood could possibly have killed more people than the Hiroshima Bomb?'

'Cut out the Communist propaganda, you hypocrite! The Americans should have taken control of the whole world, when they had the secret of the atom bomb all to themselves. Their pussy-footing was a terrible mistake.'

'And you cut out your nonsense. And tell me something: are you back on the old terms with Mariana again?'

'You must be mad,' he snorted. 'I'm too old. Broken by age and politics. I'd need a miracle for that sort of thing. And as for her, she's a woman only in the abstract. But what about you? Have you forgotten all your old escapades? The scandal-sheets of the thirties were full of them; your chasing every skirt—or rather *melaya*—in Sharia Mohammad Aly.'[18]

I laughed, and made no comment.

'Have you returned to the Faith?' he asked.

'What about you? Sometimes I think you must find it hard to believe in anything.'

'How can I deny God,' he asked angrily, 'when I am deep in His hell?'

*   *   *

'People like you were made for hell! Get out! God will never bless any of your work! Get out of this sanctified house, as Iblis[19] was turned out of God's grace!'

*   *   *

The clock in the hall struck midnight. The wind whistled in the air-shaft. I sat sunk in my warm armchair, too lazy to go to bed, thinking in my loneliness: 'What good is remorse after eighty?' Abruptly, the door opened and Tolba Marzuq stood there without knocking.

'I beg your pardon. I saw the light. Thought you were still awake.'

I looked at him in surprise. It was obvious that he was drunk.

'Do you know how much I used to spend every month just on medicine,' he asked, 'on vitamins, hormones, perfume, creams—and so forth?' He jerked his head sideways at every item.

I waited for him to go on, until he closed his eyes, as though exhausted by the effort, then went out and shut the door.

The marquee was full of people; the surrounding square was like Judgement Day. Fireworks burst in the air, crackling light turning night into day, to declare the Prophet's Birth. The Rolls Royce drew up slowly and stopped before the marquee. The crowd, fellow members of the Dimirdashiyya,[20] rushed forward to receive Tolba Marzuq, the Under-secretary of State, as he stepped out—followers of the Way, who had contrived somehow to reconcile love for the Prophet with love for His British Excellency,

14

*the Resident. His Other Excellency, the owner of the Rolls Royce,
saw me in the crowd and deliberately turned his back.* And that
night, Tolba, they said that you'd turned up just as you've turned
up tonight—drunk. *And then the Master of Song was called to the
middle of the tent to begin the evening with 'O Ultimate Heaven'.
He sang on and on into the small hours until he finally gave us
'Would that mine eyes might see you every day,' and ravished us
all.*

A wonderful memory; when it was exactly I can't remember,
but it must have been before the death of my own great master, or
I would not have enjoyed myself as I did.

*   *   *

I was sitting by myself in the *pension* when the bell rang. I opened
the judas as Madame always did and met a pair of eyes that belonged to a pretty face, a sun-tanned face, framed in the black
scarf of a *fellaha*,[21] with features full of character and an expectant
look that went instantly to the heart.

'Who are you?'

'I'm Zohra,' she said simply, as if she were somehow sure I'd
know the name.

'And what can I do for you, Zohra?' I asked, smiling.

'I want Madame Mariana.'

I opened the door and she came in, carrying a little bundle. She
looked around enquiringly.

'Where is Madame?'

'She'll be here soon. Sit down.'

She sat on the edge of a chair with her bundle on her knees. I
went back to my seat. A strong graceful figure, a very charming
young face. I tried to draw her into conversation.

'Your name is Zohra?'

'Yes, Zohra Salama.'

'Where do you come from?'

'Zayadiyya, Beheira.'[22]

'You have an appointment with Madame?'

'No. I just came to see her.'

'She knows you, of course?'

'Oh yes.'

I regarded her. She was attractive. I hadn't felt so good for ages.

'You've lived here long?'

'I've never lived in Alexandria, but I used to come here often
with my father before he died.'

15

'How did you come to know Madame?'

'Father used to sell her cheese and butter and chickens, and once in a while I'd come with him.'

'I see. You've taken up your father's business?'

'No.' She turned her gaze away towards the screen. I could see she did not want to say any more. Respecting her privacy, I refrained from questioning her further, liking her the more for her reserve and admiring her in silence.

I kissed her thin, leathery hand.

'With your blessings, I am now a man you can well be proud of. Come with me to Cairo,' I said.

'God prosper you tenfold'—she looked at me tenderly—'But I can't leave my home. It's my whole life.' A weary old house, its walls flaking, beaten by a wind that left salt on its stones and the smell of fish in heaps on the shore at Anfushi.

'But you're all alone here.'

'The Creator of day and night is always with me.'[23]

The bell rang and Zohra went and opened the door. 'Zohra!' Mariana cried. 'What a surprise!' The girl kissed her hand, her face beaming at the warm welcome. 'It is good to see you. God rest your father's soul. You're married?'

'No!'

'Impossible!' Laughing, Mariana turned to me as she took Zohra inside. 'Her father was a truly good man, Monsieur Amer.'

I felt a surge of paternal tenderness towards the girl.

* * *

'Now I can relax,' Madame informed Tolba and me that evening. 'Zohra will help me.'

I was seized by mixed feelings of pleasure and anxiety. 'Has she come to work as a maid?'

'Yes—and why not? She'll be better off here anyway.'

'But ...'

'But what? She used to rent half a *feddan* and work it herself. What do you think of that?'

'Good. But why did she leave her village?'

Mariana gave me a long look before saying: 'She ran away.'

'Ran away?'

'Did they take her for a feudalist as well?' said Tolba, chuckling.

'Her grandfather wanted to marry her to an old man, who probably needed her as a nurse. You can guess the rest.'

'But it's extremely serious for her,' I said gravely. 'The village won't forgive her.'

'She has no one but her grandfather and a married elder sister.'

'What if they find out that she's here?'

'They may. But what does it matter?'

'Aren't you afraid?'

'She's not a child, you know. What have I done? Taken her in, and given her some honest work.' She said finally, with a note of determination: 'Monsieur Amer, I shall stick to that girl.'

'I shall cling to duty as long as I live. Might is not right. Let them do their utmost.'

* * *

She showed her what to do and Zohra seemed to learn very quickly. Mariana was delighted.

'She's wonderful,' she confided to me happily. 'She's strong and intelligent, understands everything once I tell her. I'm in luck, really.'

A little later, she consulted me. 'What do you think? Five pounds a month above her board and clothes?'

I said it was fair, but begged Madame not to dress Zohra in modern city clothes.

'Why? You don't want her to go around in those peasant rags?'

'My dear, she's very good-looking. Think . . .'

'I'll keep my eyes open. And she's a good girl.'

And so, after years of concealment under an ankle-length *gallabiyya*,[24] Zohra appeared in a cotton frock cut to a size that did justice to her charming figure. Her hair was washed with kerosene, parted in the middle and hung down her back in two thick plaits. Tolba gave her a lengthy stare, then whispered, 'Next summer we'll probably find her in the Genevoise or the Monte Carlo.'

'Oh, for God's sake,' I said.

As he passed her on his way to the door, he asked her jokingly: 'Do you have any French ancestors, Zohra?'

She looked after him doubtfully. It was clear she didn't like him.

'He's only joking,' I said when she turned to me. 'Take it as a compliment.' I added with a smile: 'I too am one of your admirers.'

She smiled gently back. I was pleased to see that she liked and trusted me. I had been kind to her and we had become friends.

When Madame invited her, after she'd finished her work, to sit with us as we gathered around the radio, she would choose a seat near the screen, a little apart, and follow our conversation with grave attention. One evening, supposing that we had not heard it from Mariana, she told us her story.

'My brother-in-law wanted to take advantage of my situation, so I farmed my piece of land on my own.'

'Wasn't it difficult for you, Zohra?'

'No, I'm strong, thank God. No one ever got the better of me in business. In the field or at the market.'

Tolba laughed. 'But men are interested in other things, too.'

'I can stand up to them like a man, if it's called for.'

I heartily approved of this attitude.

'She's not an innocent,' added Mariana. 'She used to go every-where with her father. He was very fond of her.'

'And I loved him more than anything,' Zohra said wistfully. 'All my grandfather wants is to exploit me.'

Tolba would not let it pass. 'If you could stand up to them like a man,' he teased, 'then why did you run away?'

Mariana broke in. 'I have come to her assistance!'

'Come now, you know what villages are like, Tolba Bey,' I said. 'How they worship the grandfathers and their terrible con-servatism. She either had to run away or stay and be two-faced.'

She looked at me gratefully. She said, 'I left my land behind.'

Then Tolba remarked: 'They'll say you ran away because you had a lover, or something of the sort.'

She gave him an angry look and her face darkened like a Nile flood. She pointed her fore- and middle-fingers at him. 'I'd stick these into the eyes of anyone who dared to say a thing like that.'

'Zohra, can't you take a joke?' cried Mariana.

'He's only teasing you.' I tried to soothe her, surprised at the force of her anger. 'Where's your tact, my dear sir?' I asked Tolba.

'It's been sequestrated!'

*　　*　　*

Her eyes are as brown as honey, her cheeks are rosy and rounded and her little chin is dimpled. A child. *Barely as old as my grand-daughter. And her grandmother? Lost in the blink of an eye. Without even knowing love or marriage. Who was she? Impos-sible. Impossible even to remember what she looked like.* In my memory now are only the names of places: Bargawan, Darb al Ahmar, and the saintly shrine of Sidi Abu el Su'ud,[25] the healer of broken hearts.

*   *   *

'How long will you be staying here, sir?'

She used to bring coffee to my room every afternoon and I would make her stay until my desire to converse with her was satisfied.

'For good, Zohra.'

'And your family?'

'I have no one but you, my dear.' That made her laugh.

Her little hands were hard, her fingertips calloused, her feet large and flat. But her figure and face were lovely.

'I don't like him,' she once whispered to me about the other lodger.

'He's an old, unfortunate man. Besides,' I said charitably, 'he's sick.'

'He thinks he's still living in the days of the pashas. And he acts like one.'

At her words my mind went spinning back round the whole circumference of the last hundred years.

They refuse to visit the Minister of Justice because he's an effendi and not a pasha or a bey?'

'My dear sir, members of the bench have their self-esteem.'

'It is because I am above all a fellah, and they are Circassians.[26] Listen. They have always jeered at me because I am a leader of the people. And my answer has always been that I am proud to lead the rabble in their blue gallabiyyas. Mark this. They shall come, and with all due respect.'

She even learned the foreign names of all the brands of whisky she bought us at the High-Life Grocery. 'People stare and laugh when I ask for these.' In the silence of my heart I blessed ... her simplicity.

*   *   *

What a noise! The voices were familiar, but loud and sharp. I wondered what was happening outside.

As I got out of bed and put on my dressing-gown, the clock was striking five in the afternoon. Out in the hall I saw Tolba disappearing into his room, wringing his hands. Zohra was hunched in a chair, her face puckered, on the verge of tears. In front of her stood Mariana, obviously distressed.

'What's happening?'

'Zohra is so suspicious, Amer Bey.'

'He asked me to massage him,' the girl shot back roughly, reassured by my presence.

'You don't understand,' Mariana put in. 'You know he's an invalid. He needs massage for treatment. He used to go to Europe every year for the cure. You don't have to do anything you don't like.'

'I never heard of such things,' the girl said angrily. 'I went into his room in good faith and there he was lying on his face almost naked.'

'Calm down, Zohra. He's an old man, older then your father. You just don't understand. Go and wash your face and forget it.'

Left to ourselves in the hall we sat on the ebony settee. Madame broke the heavy silence.

'It was his request and I don't believe he meant any harm.'

'Mariana,' I said significantly, 'there's never an end to folly.'

'Don't you trust him? You know he's an old man.'

'They have their own kind of folly.'

'I thought she could earn some good money, instead of his going off to pay a professional.'

'You know she's a *fellaha*. And after all you've taken responsibility for her.'

Tolba joined us, putting on an innocent air and remarking scornfully: 'Once a peasant, always a peasant.'

'Leave her alone,' I said. 'Let her die as God made her.'

He was clearly offended. 'She's a wildcat. Don't let that dress and Mariana's grey cardigan fool you. She's a savage.'

Poor Zohra, how sorry I am for you. Now I know how lonely you must be. This *pension* is no place for you; and Mariana, your protectress, would have no qualms at eating you up on the first available occasion.

'God's wisdom!' said Tolba, after his first drink.

'Watch out, Tolba Bey,' said Mariana, glad to change the subject. 'Don't blaspheme.'

'Tell me, my dear,' he said, pointing to the little statue of the Madonna, 'why did God allow His Son to die on the Cross?'

'To redeem us,' she said gravely, 'or we should have been damned.'

'You mean we aren't damned anyway?' He threw back his head and laughed, looking in my direction for encouragement, but I ignored him. Then he nudged me with his elbow. 'You must help me make it up with Zohra, you old fox!'

* * *

A new guest?

Something about the well-formed dark features gives away his peasant origin. He is solidly built, rather dark, with a strong, piercing look; about thirty years old, I should guess. Mariana motions him to take a seat at the breakfast table.

'Monsieur Sarhan el-Beheiry,' she says, introducing us, and asking him, if he doesn't mind, to tell us more about himself.

'Deputy Head Accountant at the Alexandria Textile Mills,' he says with a strong country accent.

When he leaves, Mariana confides happily: 'Another lodger, on the same terms.'

Not more than a week later came Hosni Allam, a little younger than Sarhan, also as a permanent resident. Big and husky, he carried himself like a wrestler. Mariana said he belonged to one of the old country families of Tanta.[27]

Then came Mansour Bahi, an announcer with the Alexandria Broadcasting Service, twenty-five years old. I was charmed by his delicate, fine features. There was something childish perhaps even feminine, about his face. One could see at once that he was rather withdrawn, an introvert.

All the rooms were now occupied and Mariana was very happy. My heart, hungry for contact, warmed to the new arrivals. 'It's good to have young people around. I hope they won't be bored with our decrepit company.'

'Well, at least they're not students,' said Mariana.

We did not get acquainted any further until the first Thursday of the Umm Kulthum season, when I learned from Mariana that they would join us in the evening to listen to the concert on the radio. How pleasant. An evening of youth and music.

* * *

They had ordered a kebab supper and a bottle of whisky. We gathered around the radio and Zohra waited on us, moving lightly. It was a cold night, but the wind was hushed. Zohra said the sky outside was so clear you could count the stars. The drinks went round and she sat apart, next to the screen, her eyes smiling. Only Tolba Marzuq was unable to put away all anxiety: a few days before he had confided to me: 'This place is becoming a hell!' He was suspicious of strangers, certain that they knew his history and the circumstances of his ordeal, either from the papers or through Mansour Bahi.

Mariana had of course got all the information she could about the young men. 'Monsieur Sarhan el Beheiry is one of the Beheiry family.' I had never heard the name before nor, obviously, had Tolba Marzuq. 'A friend of his recommended the Pension when he learned that Monsieur Sarhan wanted to give up his flat.'

'And Hosni Allam?'

'He's one of the Allams of Tanta.' It seemed to me that Tolba knew the family, but he made no comment. 'He has a hundred *feddans*,' she added, as proudly as if she herself were the owner. 'The revolution hasn't touched him,' she went on, as joyous as someone about to be rescued at sea. 'He's come to Alexandria to start a business.'

'Why don't you cultivate your land?' Sarhan asked him when he heard that piece of information.

'It's been let.'

'You should say instead that you've never laid a hand on a hoe or a spade in your life!' mocked Sarhan. The three of them roared, but Hosni's own laugh was loudest.

'As for this young man,' said Mariana, indicating Mansour Bahi, 'he's the brother of an old friend, one of the best police chiefs I've ever known in this city.'

Tolba's cheeks turned pale.

'And before he left,' Mariana went on, 'he advised this young man to come and stay with me.'

When the others were busy drinking, Tolba leaned over and whispered: 'We've landed in a nest of spies.'

'Anti-social behaviour is out of date,' I said. 'Don't be silly.'

Whereupon politics erupted into the gathering.

'But the country has changed beyond recognition,' Sarhan was saying passionately, as he argued on behalf of the government's land reforms, his voice rising and falling in proportion to the amount of food he had in his mouth. 'And the working class! I spend my life among them. You should come to the mill and see for yourselves.'

Mansour Bahi (the quietest of the young men, though even so

he would sometimes burst out laughing, just like the others) asked him, 'Are you really in politics then?'

'Of course. I was a member of the Liberation Organization and then the National Union. Now I'm on the Committee of Twenty and I'm also an elected member of the Company Board,[28] representing the staff.'

'Were you in politics before the Revolution?'

'No.'

'I support the Revolution wholeheartedly,' said Hosni Allam. 'My people consider me a rebel.'

'Why not?' replied Mansour. 'The Revolution hasn't touched you.'

'That's not the reason. Even the poorer members of our class may not support it.'

'My own conviction,' Mansour remarked, 'is that the Revolution has been more lenient with its enemies than it ought to have been.'

Apparently Tolba thought that in the circumstances his silence might be held against him. 'I've been badly hit,' he started. 'It would be sheer hypocrisy to deny that I've been hurt. But it would also be selfish to deny that what they have done was necessary!'

Mariana did not drink. She took some of the kebab and a glass of warm milk. 'It's a pity Umm Kulthum starts so late,' she complained, even though the young men were helping us pass the time in a very agreeable fashion while we waited.

Mansour Bahi turned and spoke suddenly to me. 'I know a great deal of your brilliant past.' I was overcome with a childish pleasure: to be able to recall my youth! 'I often look through the back numbers of old newspapers for a programme I write.' Delighted, I encouraged him to say more. 'You go back a long way. You made a major contribution to the political currents of the past—the People's Party, the National Party. The Wafd, the Revolution.'

I seized this opportunity and took him with me at once on a voyage back into history, leading him to events that should never have been forgotten. We reviewed the parties one by one, the pros and cons of the People's Party and the National Party; the Wafd and how it resolved long-standing contradictions—and why, after all that, I had shifted away into independence, why I supported the Revolution.

'But you weren't interested in the basic social problem.'

'I grew up in al-Azhar. Naturally I sought a compromise, a marriage of East and West.'

'But isn't it strange that you should have attacked both the Moslem Brotherhood and the Communists?'

'No. It was a puzzling period of conflicting opposites. Then came the Revolution, to absorb what was best in each.'

'So your dilemma is solved now?'

I said yes, but in fact what was in my mind was only my private dilemma, which no party or revolution could solve, and I sent up a lonely prayer. Then the hour struck. And with it I gave up my distress to a sea of song, hoping it would help resolve the conflicts in my soul, entreating that it would instil peace and love and purge my anguish in melody, bringing the supreme pleasure of insight to my heart and mind, which would both soften and sweeten the bitter obduracy of life.

Haven't you heard? The Cabinet met in the houseboat that belongs to Munira al-Mahdia, the prima donna.

It was almost dawn when I retired to my room. Tolba joined me there, to ask what I'd thought of his little speech.

'Wonderful.' My voice sounded strange, for I had removed my false teeth.

'Do you think anyone believed me?'

'It doesn't matter.'

'I'd better look for other accommodation.'

'Nonsense.'

'For me to hear people praise these murderous regulations is enough to bring on another stroke.'

'You'd better get used to it.'

'As you have?'

I smiled. 'We've always been different, you know.'

'I wish you terrible dreams,' he remarked as he left.

*   *   *

'These young men are so attractive and well-to-do.'

Mariana often expressed her satisfaction with her young lodgers. Zohra's chores multiplied, but she rose to it all with re-doubled energy.

'I can't trust any of them,' Tolba complained.

'Not even Hosni Allam?' Mariana enquired.

But he did not seem to listen. 'Sarhan el-Beheiry is the most dangerous. He's made good under the Revolution. Let alone the

Beheiry family, of which no one has ever heard. Everyone in the province of Beheira, is a Beheiry, anyway. Even Zohra is Zohra el-Beheiry.'

I laughed and so did Mariana. Zohra passed us on her way out, wearing Madame's grey cardigan and a blue scarf she had recently bought with her own money. She was as graceful as a wild flower.

'Mansour Bahi is very intelligent, don't you think?' I asked. 'He doesn't talk much, but just goes quietly to work. A true child of the Revolution.'

'Why should he or anyone else go along with the Revolution?'

'You speak as if there were no peasants, no workers, no youth in the land.'

'The Revolution has stolen the property of a few and the liberty of all.'

'You speak of liberty in the old sense,' I said. 'And when you were top dog you didn't even show respect for that!'

*　　*　　*

Leaving the bathroom, I caught sight of two figures in the dim passage, Zohra and Sarhan whispering to each other. At that moment he raised his voice to give her instructions about his laundry. I went to my room as if I hadn't noticed anything, but I was filled with anxiety. How could Zohra live in peace in a place full of young men? When she brought my afternoon coffee, I asked her where she spent her free afternoon on Sundays.

She beamed. 'I go to the cinema.'

'On your own?'

'With Madame.'

'God keep you,' I said gently.

She smiled. 'You worry over me as if I were a child.'

'You are a child, Zohra.'

'No. When I have to, I can take care of myself as well as any man.'

I set my old face nearer her pretty young one. 'Zohra, these young men are always ready to play, but when it comes to serious intentions . . .' I snapped my fingers.

'My father told me all about that.'

'I won't pretend I'm not very fond of you. So I'm concerned.'

'I understand. I haven't met anyone like you since my father. I'm fond of you, too.'

I had never heard the words said so sweetly, and they were

words that, if it had not been for an accusation made in stupidity, and which no man alive had the right to make, I might have heard from the lips of dozens of children and grandchildren of my own. *That white transparent veil! The old woman nips out from the door in the little alley: 'Come on, it has stopped raining.' The girl in the white veil follows, stepping carefully on the slippery stones.* Has time dimmed all the details of that beautiful face, leaving only the deep impression? *I stand to one side and I whisper: 'God be praised for creating such beauty.' While my heart is still pounding, I say to myself: 'Take the decision, put your trust in God! The sooner the better!'*

*　　　*　　　*

I am alone with Mariana, who sits beneath the Madonna, her blue eyes dark with thought. It has been raining steadily since noon, the clouds shaken by occasional rolls of thunder. Mariana speaks.

'Monsieur Amer, I smell something fishy!'

'What?' I ask warily.

'Zohra,' she says; and then, after a pause, 'Sarhan el-Beheiry.'

My heart contracts. 'What do you mean?'

'You know exactly what I mean.'

'But the girl . . .'

'I have an instinct about these things.'

'My dear Mariana, she's a good honest girl.'

'Maybe, but I don't like people going on behind my back!'

Of course. Either Zohra stays 'honest' or she works for you. I know you through and through, old woman.

*　　　*　　　*

I have dreams, during my siesta, about 1919, that bloody uprising,[29] and the British soldiers afterwards forcing their way into the Azhar. I open my eyes with a brain full of shouting demonstrators, the smack of rifles and the thud of bullets. There are loud voices in the entrance hall. I put on my dressing-gown and hurry out. Others are there, watching, but Sarhan is adjusting his collar and tie with an angry sneer on his face. And there is Zohra, pale with anger, her breast heaving, her dress torn at the neckline, while Hosni Allam in his dressing-gown is just going out the door with a strange woman who screams and curses—and who just before the door closes spits in Sarhan's face.

26

'My *pension* has a good name!' Mariana shouts, 'I won't stand for this sort of thing. No, no, no!'

I am still half asleep. When there are only the three of us left, I ask Tolba Marzuq what happened.

'I haven't the faintest idea. I arrived on the scene only just before you did.'

Mariana disappears into Sarhan's room; for an explanation no doubt.

'It seems the Beheiry boy is quite a Don Juan.'

'What makes you think so?'

'Didn't you see her spit in his face?'

'Who was she, anyway?'

'Just a woman.' He grins. 'Come for her runaway boyfriend, I suppose.'

Zohra comes back, still upset. 'I opened the door for Monsieur Sarhan,' she tells us, though we haven't asked her anything, 'and there was this woman following him. He didn't see her. Then they started fighting.'

Mariana returns from Sarhan's room. 'The girl was his fiancée. Or so I understand.'

We all understand. But it is Tolba Marzuq who slyly puts the question:

'Then what's Zohra got to do with all this?'

'I tried to break it up and she turned on me.'

'You've got a fine fist, Zohra!'

'Let's not speak of it any more,' I beg them.

*　　*　　*

Bismallah al Rahman al Rahim.
Ta. Sin. Mim.
These are revelations of the Scripture that
*   maketh plain.*
We narrate unto thee somewhat of the story
*   of Moses and Pharaoh with truth for folk*
*   who believe.*
Lo! Pharaoh exalted himself in the earth and
*   made its people castes. A tribe among them*
*   he oppressed, killing their sons and sparing*
*   their women. Lo! he was of those who work corruption.*
And we desired to show favour unto those who
*   were oppressed in the earth, and to make*
*   them examples and to make them the inheritors!*[30]

27

Someone is knocking. Mariana comes in smiling and sits on the backless stool where I sometimes rest my feet. The wind is howling in the air-shaft and I am swathed in my dressing-gown. The room is very quiet and dim, drowsing in a light that does not reveal the time of day.

'Haven't you heard?' She is stifling a laugh.

I close my book and put it on the bedside table. 'Good news, my dear?'

'Zohra's going to school!'

I do not understand.

'Really, She's made up her mind. She asked permission to stay away for an hour in the afternoon. To take lessons.'

'Amazing.'

'She's arranged it with a schoolmistress who lives on the fifth floor. A young teacher who'll give her private lessons.'

I repeat, 'It's amazing.'

'I didn't object, but I'm afraid she's going to spend all her wages on it.'

'That's thoughtful of you, Mariana. But I'm really and truly amazed.'

When Zohra brought me my afternoon coffee, I said; 'You've been keeping secrets from me, you naughty child.'

'I keep no secrets from you,' she answered shyly.

'What about this decision to study? What made you think of it?'

'All girls go to school now. The streets are full of them.'

'But you never thought of it before.'

'It's your fault,' she smiled. 'You said I was much prettier than they are and there was no reason why they should read and write while I stayed illiterate.' She went on looking up brightly at me.

'But that isn't all.'

'What else is there?'

'Well ... there's our friend Sarhan el-Beheiry.' She blushed. 'Learning to read and write is a wonderful idea. As for Sarhan ...'

'Yes?' She asked, when I hesitated.

'Young men are ambitious.'

'We're all the children of Adam and Eve,' she replied tartly.

'True, but ...'

'Times have changed. Haven't they?'

'Yes, they have. They have indeed. But young men haven't changed.'

'When I learn to read and write,' she said thoughtfully, 'I'll try and learn some profession. Like dressmaking, perhaps.'

I was afraid I might hurt her feelings if I said much more.

'Does he love you?' She lowered her eyes. 'May God bless you and bring you happiness!'

From time to time I would help her with her lessons, that mysterious world of letters and figures. All the lodgers learned of her decision and discussed it at length. No one laughed at her, at least not to her face. They all liked her, I suppose, each in his own way.

Tolba Marzuq exercised his usual penetration. 'The best solution to her problem would be a new lodger. A film producer or something. What do you think of that?'

I cursed his dirty mind.

Late one afternoon when I took my usual seat in the hall, I saw an unfamiliar girl sitting next to Zohra on the settee—obviously the teacher, good-looking and well dressed. She had agreed to come down to her pupil because there were visitors in her own flat. Mariana had of course put all the questions she could. Later she told us that the young lady lived with her parents and had a brother who worked in Saudi Arabia.

Afterwards the teacher came frequently to the *pension*. She said she was pleased with her new pupil's perseverance.

One afternoon, as she brought my coffee, Zohra seemed depressed. I asked her how she was.

'I'm as fit as a mule.'

'And the lessons?'

'Nothing to complain of.'

'Then it's our friend Beheiry,' I suggested with concern. For a moment neither of us said a word, as if we were listening to the rain. 'I can't stand seeing you unhappy. You must tell me what's happened.'

'I believe you,' she said gratefully.

'What's wrong?'

'Well, I suppose luck just isn't on my side.'

'I warned you from the first day.'

'It's not that easy, you know.' She looked miserably at me. 'What can I do? I love him. What can I do?'

'Has he deceived you?'

'No! He loves me too. But he always speaks of obstacles.'

'But when a man's in love . . .'

'He *does* love me! Yet he keeps talking about these obstacles.'

'But they're not your fault. You have to be sure where you stand.'

'What's the good of knowing what I should do when I couldn't bring myself to do it?'

*   *   *

'*My dear Pasha, how could you?*'

'*I had no alternative. I needed the loan from the Agricultural Credit Bank. Their terms were very clear-cut. I had either to quit the Wafd or be ruined.*'

'*But many have chosen that latter alternative.*'

'*Shut up!*' he shouted. '*You don't own one square inch of land! You have neither son nor daughter! And even though I have been beaten and imprisoned at Kasr el Nil Barracks,*[31] *my daughter is dearer to me than either this world or the next!*'

*   *   *

'Come with me,' Mariana whispered. 'Zohra's people are here.'

I went out with her. Zohra's sister and brother-in-law were there, the girl herself standing proudly in the middle of the room. The man was speaking,

'It's all right that you came to Madame. As for your running away, though . . .'

'You shamed us,' her sister cut in, 'all over Zayediyya.'

'It's none of anybody's business,' said Zohra bitterly.

'If only your grandfather could be here!'

'I answer to no one, now my father's dead.'

'How dare you! He only wanted to marry you to a good man!'

'He wanted to sell me.'

'God forgive you. Come along! Get your things ready.'

'I am *not* going back. Not even if the dead themselves come out of their graves.' Her brother-in-law was about to speak, but she stopped him. 'It's none of your business. I have a good job here.' She pointed to Mariana. 'I earn my living by honest work.'

It struck me that they would have liked very much to tell her what they thought of Madame, the *pension*, and the statue of the Virgin, but felt themselves unable to.

'Zohra is the daughter of a man I respected,' said Mariana. 'I treat her as a daughter and she's welcome to stay if she likes.' She looked at me, as if to prompt.

'Think, Zohra,' I said, 'and make your choice.'

'I am *not* going back.'

Their mission was a failure. As he left with his wife, however, the man said to Zohra, 'You deserve to be killed!'

Afterwards we talked it over at length until Zohra said, 'What do you really think I should do?'

'I wish you could go back to your village.'

'Go back to misery?'

'I said "*I wish you could*"—that is, go back and be happy.'

'I love the land and the village, but I hate that misery.' And when Mariana went out of the room, she said sadly: 'Here is where love is. Education. Cleanliness. And hope.'

I could understand her feelings. I too had left the village with my father; and after that, like her, I had loved the village but could not bear to live there. I had educated myself, as she would like to do, and I had been wrongly accused and many people had said, as they had just said to her, that I should be killed. And like her again, I had been entranced by love, education, cleanliness, hope. May your fortune be better than mine, Zohra!

* * *

Autumn is wearing on to its end. But Alexandrian weather, which knows no rule, blesses us with a bright warm morning; Ramleh Square is radiant with sunlight pouring out of a pure azure sky. Mahmoud Abu el Abbas, the newspaper-seller, smiles at me as I stand in front of his stall, which is adorned with the covers of magazines and books.

'Sir,' he begins, while I suppose there's been some mistake in our account, for he stands there, tall and thickset, saying; 'You live in the Pension Miramar?'

'Yes.' I nod.

'I beg your pardon. But there is a girl called Zohra.'

'Yes?' I am suddenly attentive.

'Where are her people?'

'Why do you ask?'

'I beg your pardon, but I want to propose to her.'

I reflect for a moment. 'Her people are in the country. I think she's quarrelled with them. Have you spoken to her about it?'

'She comes here to buy papers, but she doesn't encourage me to talk.'

The same evening he paid Mariana a visit and asked for Zohra's hand. Mariana spoke to her, but the girl refused him on the spot.

'You've spoilt her, Mariana,' commented Tolba when he heard the story. 'Cleaning her up and dressing her in modern clothes won't do her much good. She mixes with fine young men and her head's turned. She'll come to no good. You mark my words.'

When she came with my afternoon coffee, we discussed the matter.

'You should have given it more thought'

'But you know everything!' she protested.

'Still, there's no harm in considering a serious proposal.'

She said reproachfully, 'You think I'm too humble to hope for anything better, don't you?'

'No!' I flung out my hand. 'I just think he'd make you a suitable husband, that's all.'

'It'd be the same as going back to the village.' I did not like that answer. 'You see, I overheard him speaking to another newsboy once,' she explained. 'He hadn't noticed me standing there. He was saying: "All women have one thing in common. They're cuddly little animals without brains or religion, and the only way to keep them from going wild is to leather them every day!" ' She challenged me. 'Am I to blame if I refuse such a man?'

I had nothing to say. And though I pretended to be disturbed, I felt an unbounded admiration for the girl. I thought to myself, *no more old men's advice*! Saad Zaghloul always used to listen to what they had to say, then followed the counsel of the young. God protect you, Zohra.

*   *   *

'Great things are happening right under your nose, old man,' Tolba Marzuq said, grinning slyly. We were sitting alone in the *pension*, listening to the beating rain.

'What's the matter?' I expected bad news.

'The Don Juan from Beheira is preparing another coup.' I showed concern for Zohra's sake. 'He's changed his quarry. Aiming at something else, in fact.'

'Forget your own pleasures for a minute and speak plainly.'

'It's the teacher's turn now.'

'Zohra's teacher?'

'Exactly! I caught surreptitious looks going back and forth above the diligent student's head. I'm quite an expert, you know.'

'Papa Amer, watch out for a most entertaining comedy at the Miramar!'

'You're simply depraved.'

I was determined not to believe a word of what he said. But I was worried. The same evening Hosni Allam told us about a fight between Sarhan el-Beheiry and Mahmoud Abu el Abbas the news-agent in the square. They'd come to blows, and people had hardly been able to separate them. I knew at once what had been behind the quarrel.

'They hit each other until people had to force them apart,' said Hosni.

'Did you see them fight?' asked Tolba.

'No, but I knew about it shortly afterwards.'

'Did they go to the police?' Mariana wanted to know.

'No, the whole thing ended in a lot of name-calling—and threats.'

Sarhan said nothing about this incident and none of us made any reference to it. The thought of Sarhan and the teacher depressed me. Poor Zohra.

*   *   *

' "And when are the fair ever faithful? My only comfort is tears!" '
We clap and cheer for several encores and he sings until the break of dawn. I am full that night of youth and strength and food. Drink, too. But the heart, alone, endures its secret chagrin.

*   *   *

Deep in sleep, in the lost hours of night, I had dreamt of my father's death. I saw them carry the body out of the arcade of the mosque of Sidi Abu el Abbas, where death had found him, and take him home. I was weeping and I could hear my mother's shrieks of mourning and they went on and on until I opened my eyes. *Good God, what could be going on outside? Was it the same thing again?* The *pension* had become a battlefield, though by the time I left my room everything was over.

When she saw me Mariana came running. 'No! No! To hell with the whole lot of them!' she cried when we were in my room. I looked at her out of heavy-lidded eyes and I listened to the story. She'd been awakened by the sound of a fight and gone out to find Sarhan el-Beheiry and Hosni Allam exchanging blows in the corridor.

'Hosni Allam?'

'Yes, why not? They're all stark mad.'

'But why?'

'Apparently something happened that I didn't see. I was asleep, too.'

'What about the girl?'

33

'Zohra says Hosni came home dead drunk and that he tried to . . .'

'No!'

'I believe her, Monsieur Amer,' said Mariana.

'I do, too. But Hosni didn't seem interested in her.'

'But we can't notice everything, Monsieur Amer. Anyway, Sarhan woke up at the right time. Why must these things happen?' She massaged her throat, as if to rub off the pain of shouting. 'No,' she repeated, 'to hell with them.'

'Anyway,' I said with annoyance, 'Hosni should go.'

But she made no comment; she did not seem to like the idea and went out with a disturbed look on her face.

When Zohra came in the next afternoon we just looked at each other.

'I am sorry you've been through all this, Zohra.'

'They're not gentlemen.'

'The truth is you shouldn't be here.'

'I can always defend myself. Which I've done.'

'But they won't leave you in peace. Living here isn't the right thing for a good girl like you.'

'There are rats everywhere. Even in our village.'

*　　　*　　　*

I was confined to the *pension* for several days by cold, wind, and rain. Though we all kept to our rooms the elements seemed to follow us there: rain rattled at the windows, the walls shook with thunder, and lightning flashed ominously, while the wind howled like a jinn.

When I finally went out, it was another Alexandria that received me, the fury past, calm again, giving itself to the clear golden rays of the sun. I looked out at the waves in their nonchalant succession, the little cloud-puffs dotted across the sky. Then I went and took my seat in the Trianon and ordered my *café au lait* as I used to in the good old days with Gharably Pasha, Sheikh Darwish and Madame Lobraska—the only Frank I ever made love to, once upon a time when I was drowned in women. Tolba Marzuq sat with me for a while, then left for the lobby of the Windsor, where he was meeting an old friend. I saw Sarhan coming towards me. He shook my hand and sat down.

'I'm glad I've met you here,' he said. 'I must say goodbye. I may not see you when I check out this afternoon.'

I was really surprised. 'Are you leaving the *pension?*'

'Yes, I am. I'd have been really sorry to go without saying good-bye to you.'

I thanked him for his kind thoughts and would have liked to ask him a few questions, but he gave me no chance. He waved to someone, shook my hand and left. What about Zohra? Depressed, disturbed, I sighed to myself.

* * *

He clutched at the bars as he listened to the verdict. Then he shouted at the top of his voice: 'Proud of yourself, you bastards? Are you happy, Naima, you officers' whore?'[32]

* * *

I found Mariana, Tolba Marzuq, and Zohra in the hall. The atmosphere was heavy with gloom.

'That hypocrite Sarhan has shown his true colours.'

'I met him at the Trianon and he said he's leaving,' I muttered.

'In fact I turned him out. He assaulted her shamelessly,' said Mariana, indicating Zohra with a motion of her head. 'Then he announced that he's leaving to marry the school mistress upstairs.'

I glanced at Tolba and he looked back with a mischievous smile. 'So he's finally made up his mind to get married.'

'I never really liked him,' said Mariana. 'I could see through him from the start. A young man of no principles. Monsieur Mansour Bahi tried to talk to him and they started fighting as well. I told him to get out on the spot.'

I looked at Zohra. What a monstrous thing! The game was up and the villain had gone unpunished. I was gripped by an anger I hadn't felt since the bitter old days of political struggle.

'He's a swine,' I told Zohra. 'Don't waste any regrets on him.'

When we were alone I told Tolba I wished she would marry Mahmoud Abu el Abbas.

'What Mahmoud?' he said provocatively. 'Can't you see that she's lost something irretrievable?' I protested, though I felt stunned. 'You old fool! Can't you see what's been going on under your nose?'

'Zohra isn't like that!'

'God bless you for an innocent!' I hated him. But I couldn't help beginning to doubt the poor girl. 'Madame was the first to draw

35

my attention to their relationship. Though I could have guessed myself.'

'She's a wicked woman,' I said angrily.

'But Madame, you understand, is most eager to act as her protector—or exploiter.'

'No. She won't. I'll see to that.'

When she came into my room in the afternoon, the girl was terribly downcast. She begged me pathetically not to remind her of my earlier advice. I said I wouldn't—but what was she going to do?

'I hope you won't give up the lessons.'

'No. I'll find another teacher.' Her voice was joyless, but determined enough.

'If you need any help, I . . .'

She bent and kissed my shoulder biting her underlip to hold back her tears. I stretched out my veined and leathery old hand until it rested on her young black hair.

'God bless you, Zohra.'

*   *   *

That night I kept more or less to my room, giving in to a sense of complete malaise, so fatigued that I was unable to go out for some days thereafter. Mariana kept pressing me to pull my strength together. 'We must celebrate the New Year,' she urged. 'Shall we go to the Monseigneur as Tolba Bey suggests, or shall we celebrate it here?'

'Here would be better, my dear.'

I didn't really care. How often had I celebrated it at Sault's, Groppi's, Alf Leila and Lipton Gardens! And one year I'd spent it in the military prison at the Citadel.[38]

On the morning of the third day of my seclusion, Mariana rushed in, extremely upset. 'Have you heard the news?' she panted, sinking into an armchair. 'Sarhan el-Beheiry's been murdered.'

'What!'

'His body was found on the road to the Palma.'

Tolba Marzuq came in nervously clutching a paper. 'This is really dreadful news. It may cause a lot of trouble.'

We looked at each other and thought of all the probabilities—his first fiancée, Hosni Allam, Mansour Bahi, Mahmoud Abu el Abbas—until Madame said: 'Why, the murderer may be someone we've never heard of!'

36

'Why not?' I agreed. 'We know hardly anything about the young man.'

Madame was very anxious. 'Oh! I wish they'd find the killer soon. I hope it's no one we know. I don't want to see the face of a policeman here.'

'I hope so, too,' sighed Tolba Marzuq—doubtless for the same reason.

Madame sighed. I asked about Zohra.

'The poor girl is terribly shocked.'

'Could I possibly see her?'

'She's locked herself in her room. Totally broken down.'

We went on discussing the murder but could come to no conclusion. I closed my eyes and heard the words sing in my head:

> *Everyone that is thereon will pass away; There remaineth but the countenance of the Lord of Might and Glory. Which is it of the favours of your Lord that ye deny?*[34]

2. HOSNI ALLAM

Ferekeeko,[35] don't put the blame on me. *The face of the sea is dark, mottled, blue from stifled wrath; there is unappeased rage in the ceaseless hammering of the waves.* Revolution? Why not? To put you where you belong, you progeny of whores, to take all your money and push your noses in the mud. Sure, I'm one of you. And I know it. That, unfortunately, is something that can't be changed. 'No education,' she said, 'and a hazardous hundred *feddans.*' That's what Miss Blue-Eyes[36] said, as she slammed the door in my face and sat down behind to wait for the next prospective stud-bull to come along.

From my balcony at the Cecil I cannot see the Corniche unless I lean out over the railing. It's like being on a ship. The sea sprawls right below me. *A great blue mass, heaving, locked in as far as the fort of Sultan Qaitbay by the Corniche wall and the giant stone jetty-arm*[37] *thrusting into the sea. Frustrated, caged. These waves slopping dully landwards have a sullen blue-black look that continually promises fury.* The sea. Its guts churn with flotsam and secret death.

My room has a formal air, like our family house in Tanta. It bores me. The glory of having land is over. What we have now is the heyday of an educated rabble.

Good. Revolution, so be it! Let it cut you all down to the ground. I'm through with you, you scraps of tattered time! Don't blame me, *Ferekeeko!*

*   *   *

'How bored I am in this grand hotel of yours!' I say to Mohamed the Nubian waiter as he serves me breakfast in my room. A long-standing habit of mine, to be liberal and courteous to servants.

38

Who knows, anyway? I might need them some day.

'Will you stay in Alexandria long, sir?'

'Yes, a very long time.'

'Don't you think in that case that a *pension* would be more suitable, sir?'

I looked at him enquiringly.

'I know a more interesting and less expensive guest-house, sir. But this is just between us.' Pleasant, serviceable and treacherous, employed by one master, secretly serving another. Like so many of my dear countrymen. All right. I suppose a *pension* would be more accommodating, a more suitable place for planning a new business. The only reason I've come to the Cecil is old habit—and, let's face it, ineradicable pride.

* * *

The little judas swings open. A very pretty face. Too pretty for a servant, much too pretty for a lady. A really beautiful girl. Who will no doubt fall in love with me at first sight.

'Yes?'

A *fellaha*! How strange. At that moment, as far as I'm concerned, the Cecil could sink beneath the black waves of the sea.

'I've been sent by Mohamed Kamel at the Cecil.'

She shows me to a seat in the hall and goes inside. Meanwhile I get the feel of the place by looking at the photographs on the walls. An English officer? So. And that beauty leaning over the back of a chair? Who could she be? She is lovely, exciting. She must be an antique, though. The style of her dress leaves little doubt that she went to school with the Virgin Mary.

A brilliant, gilded old lady comes in. The landlady, of course—a typical old retired French procuress. Or maybe (let's hope!) not quite yet retired. That photograph must be a portrait of her before time did her in. Things are falling into place. It would appear that the Nubian has interpreted my boredom at the Cecil in his own way. Fine! A little preliminary diversion is always good for thinking out new plans.

'Do you have any vacant rooms, Madame?'

'You were staying at the Cecil?' She is clearly very impressed, and wishes she were forty years younger. 'How long would you like to stay?'

'A month, at least. Who knows? Maybe a year.'

'There are special terms for the summer.'

'That's all right.'

'Are you a student?'

'No. A gentleman of property.'

She brings out the register. 'Your name, please?'

'Hosny Allam.' With no education, a hazardous hundred *feddans*, and lucky enough to know nothing at all about the thing our singers call love.

*　　*　　*

A good room, violet wallpaper. The sea-view stretches as far as the eye can see, a clear blue. The curtains flutter in the autumn breeze. There is a scattered flock of clouds in the sky. And as she makes the bed, spreading sheets and a counterpane. I study the form of the *fellaha*: a well-knit, shapely body, with obvious good points. If my guess is right, she hasn't run into pregnancy or abortion yet. I'd better wait, though, until I get to know the place a little better.

'What's your name, sweetheart?'

'Zohra,' she answers stolidly.

'Bless him that named thee!' She thanks me with a grave nod. 'Are there any other guests in the place?'

'Two gentlemen and a young man like your honour.'

'What's your nickname.'

'My name is Zohra.' Polite, not at all encouraging. Too serious, that's clear. She would enhance the interior decoration of any flat I might rent in the future, though. Certainly she's more beautiful than my idiotic kinswoman, who has decided to choose a husband with the guidance of the Revolutionary Charter.[38] *Ferekeeko*, don't blame me.

'*Are you serious?*'

'*But of course, darling!*'

'*You don't even know what love is.*'

'*I want to get married, you see.*'

'*But I don't think you could possibly fall in love.*'

'*Here I am proposing to you. Doesn't that mean I love you? I'm marriageable,*' I say, trying to keep any anger in check. '*No?*'

'*What value does land have,*' she says after a moment's hesitation, '*these days?*' It serves me right for getting myself into such a degrading situation.

'*Think it over,*' I say as I go out. '*Take your time.*'

*　　*　　*

40

At breakfast I get to know the other guests. Amer Wagdi, a retired journalist—I reckon he must be eighty at least, quite tall, thin, but in very good health. There's nothing left for death to devour—a wrinkled face, sunken eyes, and sharp bones. The very sight of the man makes me detest him. I wonder how he can survive while generations of the young go on dying every day.

Tolba Marzuq is no stranger to me. I remember my uncle saying something sympathetic about the sequestration of his property, though naturally I don't bring it up. We follow all such events, the news of sequestration and confiscation, with avid interest; like the action of a horror film.

'One of the Allams of Tanta?' he asks and I nod, with secret smugness. 'I used to know your father. An excellent farmer.' Turning to Amer Wagdi, who is leaving the table, he laughs and says, 'He wasn't under the influence of those comedians of yours for long, God rest his soul. I mean the Wafdists,' he adds when he sees that I don't understand the joke.

'For all I know, he was a Wafdist,' I answer with indifference. 'At the same time the whole country was.'

'That's right. I believe you have some brothers and sisters?'

'My brother is Consul in Italy and my sister's married to our ambassador in Ethiopia.'

'And you?' His mouth twitches.

I hate him so intensely at that moment that I wish he would drown or burn. But I put on an air of not caring.

'Nothing.'

'Don't you farm your land?'

'No, it's been let. But I'm thinking of starting up a new business.'

The third lodger has been listening attentively to our conversation; so has Madame. His name is Sarhan el-Beheiry, Deputy Head of the Accounts Department at the Alexandria Textile Mills.

'What sort of business?'

'I haven't made up my mind.'

'Why don't you look for a government post? It's more secure.'

I detest him too. He has a hint of a country accent, like the smell of cooking that lingers in a badly washed pan. Would blue-eyed Mervat, I wonder, brand this mule 'uneducated', though? I doubt it. If he has the insolence to ask about my lack of a degree I'll dash this cup of tea in Dream-Boy Beheiry's[39] face.

'Where did you get all this zeal for their Revolution?'

'I believe in it, sir.'

'I don't believe you.'

'*You should.*'

'*Mervat's refusal,*' he says with a chuckle, '*would appear to have driven you out of your mind.*'

I am irritated. '*Getting married was just a passing thought.*'

He is angry, too. '*You've got your father's obstinacy. God rest his soul. But none of his good sense.*'

Something urges me to attack the Revolution in the person of this Sarhan, who is clearly an opportunist, but I manage to give way.

'Why don't you tell us about your project?' the old lady asks.

'I still haven't made up my mind.'

'You're well-off then?'

I give her a self-confident smile but make no reply. And her interest in me is obviously thereby doubled.

I leave the *pension* at the same time as Sarhan. We take the lift down together, his smiling eyes clearly inviting me to some sort of *rapprochement*, and my anger at him subsides a little. 'A government job is, generally speaking,' he says, half-consciously correcting his earlier *gaffe*, 'more secure. A private business, however, if chosen carefully . . .' The lift is there before he can finish his sentence, but his ingratiating tone needs no further explanation. He goes to the tram stop and I go to the garages, passing the Miramar Café. I remember sitting there with my uncle in the old days before the deluge. He used to come late in the afternoon to smoke the *nargileh*[40] sitting there wrapped in his cloak, like a king in disguise, in the midst of a group of senators and country notables. Yes, those were the days. He deserved what he got, though, and then some.

I drive around in my Ford, aimless except to satisfy a craving for speed. *I'd better keep up the acquaintance with this Sarhan el-Beheiry; I may find him useful some day. He has experience, and friends in the city.*

I drive fast along the Corniche—Mazarita, Chatby, Ibrahimiya, and beyond. *My nerves have been racked and they respond gratefully to the car's speed as it slashes through the cold refreshing air under a cloudy sky. The blue-sea-edged Corniche is sharp, clear-cut, scrubbed clean of the clamour and smell of summer holiday-makers.* Tanta old girl, I'll never go back to you again, except of course to cash money or sell some land! To hell with you and your memories!

I turn off at Siyouf and cut over to the boulevard running towards Abu Qir[41]—the royal road—driving faster and faster as my spirits and confidence rise. And where, I wonder sadly, are the

Frenchwomen? Where is beauty? Where is all that solid gold? I go into the Metro Cinema for the matinée and chat up a girl at the buffet in the interval. We lunch at Omar Khayyam,[42] then have a short siesta in her little flat at Ibrahimiya. By the time I get back to the *pension* at dusk, I have completely forgotten her name.

There is no one in the entrance hall. I take a shower and the cold water somehow reminds me of the pretty *fellaha*. Back in my room I order a cup of tea, just to talk to her. I give her a piece of chocolate. She hesitates a little before taking it and I press her. 'Why not? We're all one family here.'

I look her over frankly, with pleasure, and she stares back unabashed, not even looking down. Is she cunning or is she afraid?

'Are there many like you in the country?'

'Plenty.' She ignores my obvious intention

'But surely not as pretty as you?'

She thanks me for the chocolate and leaves the room. Cunning? Or scared? Well, I don't need her now. And it's only her privilege to play a little hard to get, and her due as well for me to confess that she's very beautiful. *Ferekeeko*, don't blame me!

* * *

I stare at Madame's old photograph until she asks delightedly, 'Do you like it?' She tells me the story of her first and second marriages. 'How do you find me now?'

'As lovely as ever.' I look at her veined wrists and muddy complexion.

'I've aged before my time. It's my bad health,' she says with resignation. Then all of a sudden, veering over to a new subject: 'But is it wise to risk your money on a new business?'

'Why not?'

'What if the government confiscates it?'

'There are such things as safe projects.' Guessing that she might have contemplated hauling her own money out from under the floorboards, I add playfully, 'Wouldn't it be wonderful if we were partners?'

'Me?' She laughs with pretended surprise. 'But I can hardly live on what I get from the *pension*.'

We are joined by the ancient journalist, closely wrapped up in a warm dressing-gown, and surprisingly cheerful, despite his disgusting longevity. Qalawoon, the Doddering Sultan.[43]

'The young seek adventure, the old long for security,' he says, as if to comment on both his lot and mine.

I wish him good health.

'Have you come to Alexandria to start that project you mentioned?'

'Yes.'

'And are you serious about it?'

'Well, I'm sick of doing nothing.'

Chanting, he quotes the old verse: 'Youth, leisure and worldly goods oft prove a man's undoing.' But I despise poetry, as much as I despise being told about university degrees. And what I feel towards them is the ineffable superiority of a Turcoman horseman who finds himself living among sedentary trash. Of course the winds of fortune have soured some of them enough to give them a fair amount of polish, the same winds that at the moment are blowing my class's candle out. That's just what they're like, in fact, these revolutions—like some sort of freak of nature: like hurricanes tornadoes. *I resemble someone trying to drive a car with an exhausted battery.*

A new face comes out from behind the screen, a young man I haven't met before, heading for the door. Madame invites him to sit down, introducing him as 'Monsieur Mansour Bahi'.

He works at the Alexandria Broadcasting Station. Another of those degrees. A handsome face, delicate features; rather effeminate, though. Another polished plebeian, whose diffidence tempts me to punch him in the face.

When the fellow has gone I ask Madame whether he is a resident or a transient guest.

'A resident, my dear,' she says proudly. 'I don't take transient guests.'

Zohra comes back from the market, her plastic shopping bag heavy with groceries. I look after her greedily. The town is full of women, but this girl excites me. Is it my fault, *Ferekeeko?*

'*So you've fallen in love, after all?*'

'*Not really, Aunt, but she's a fine girl. She's my cousin, and I want to get married.*'

'*At any rate, you're a young man after any girl's heart.*'

*   *   *

The evening of Umm Kulthum's concert is a magnificent occasion, even at the Pension Miramar; we drink, laugh and talk of

44

many things, including politics. But even strong drink cannot get the better of fear.

Amer Wagdi rambles on about the glory of his own past, deeds for which his own conscience must serve, alas, as the only witness; the old wreck wants to convince us that he was formerly a hero. So no one is commonplace in this damned world. And everyone sings the praises of the Revolution. Even Tolba Marzuq. So do I. Take care, I say to myself. Sarhan is an opportunist and Mansour is probably an informer. Even the ancient scribbler . . . who knows? Madame herself is probably required to keep her eyes open, in the service of security.

When Zohra comes with a bottle of soda-water I ask her: 'And you, Zohra, do you like the Revolution?'

'Oh, you should see the portrait[44] hanging on the wall in her room,' says Madame. Tacit permission for me to creep into the girl's room some night?

The whisky draws us together in a sort of familiarity, but I know it won't last, that there will never be any real friendship between me and Sarhan and Mansour; at most a transitory intimacy that will soon evaporate, just like the girl I picked up at the Metro. I remind myself that I should find some business to use up my energy and fill my time. Otherwise, who knows? I might do something stupid. Or commit some crime—a crime worthy of myself.

What is clear is that if getting married means risking another *no*, I'd prefer to remain a bachelor. And since it's impossible for me to find a suitable wife in this 'Progressive Society', I'll permit myself to look upon all womankind as my personal harem. To fill the vacancy in my future home, I'll simply find a first-class maid. Right. A maid like Zohra, and why not Zohra herself. She'll certainly accept; she'll be grateful for the chance to play the lady without the trouble of child-bearing, nursing, and all that. She's beautiful. And she'll put up with my whims, my other love affairs. How could a girl from her background do anything else? Life isn't so bad, after all, and there's plenty of fun to be wrung out of it yet.

Sarhan tells us so many jokes that we are exhausted. Even Mansour bursts out laughing, then draws back into his shell.

'Listen! Read this! A death sentence. Will the English do nothing about it? Will they let the Communists take over?'

The singing starts and they listen greedily to the wireless. I grow tense. As usual, sure, I can follow a verse or two, but I quickly get bored and distracted. There they sit, wrapped up in the music, and

45

all I feel is terrible isolation. I'm astonished to notice that Madame is as fond of Umm Kulthum as any of them. 'I've listened to her for so many years,' she explains when she observes my surprise.

Tolba Marzuq is listening intently. 'Thank God they didn't confiscate my ears, too,' he whispers to me.

As for the Doddering Sultan, he's closed his eyes, also listening. Or having a quiet snooze.

Then I steal a look at Zohra on her seat near the screen. Very charming. But is she listening too? What's she thinking? What's she hoping? Is she being tossed around by life like the rest of us? She goes away for a moment. They are all drunk with rapture, absorbed in the music. I go after her, through the passage to the washroom and playfully pull her plait of hair, whispering: 'The only thing lovelier than the music is your face.'

She steps back firmly. I try to take her into my arms, but stop short at her frigid look.

'I've waited so long, Zohra!'

With a light step, she turns away and goes back to her seat in the hall. All right, suit yourself! There are dozens like you at the big house in Tanta, you fool. Or do you think my education is lacking something too, you yokel?

I go back to the group of listeners, disguising my anger with exaggerated applause for the concert I am not following. I have a sudden impulse to speak out for once, to tell them what I really think of it, but I don't. In the interval they all scatter and I take the opportunity to leave the house.

I drive to Cleopatra:[45] it's cold and windy but I'm on fire with the whisky. I go to the house of a Maltese madame where I used to go on summer nights. She's surprised to see me out of season and it's past midnight.

'I have no one here,' she says. 'And I can't get you a woman now.' She stands in front of me in her nightgown, past fifty, fat and flabby; but a woman still, though the down on her upper lip is like a moustache.

I push her into the bedroom.

'What are you doing?' she says with surprise. 'I'm not ready.'

'It doesn't matter.'

I laugh. Nothing matters!

Later we spend another hour talking. When she hears about my business plans, she says, 'People are selling out and leaving.'

I yawn. 'I'm not starting a factory or a company.'

'Then look for some foreigner who wants to leave and buy his business.'

'Not a bad idea, but I must think it over.'

On the way back it rains heavily and I can hardly see my way through the windscreen. I'm in a rotten temper. I know I've just been wasting my time.

* * *

Pretty, in spite of the smell of cooking.

'Two pieces of sugar, please.' To stir the sugar for me she has to stay a little longer in my room. 'You were hard on me, Zohra.'

'No, you went too far.'

'I wanted to tell you how much I admire you.'

'I'm just here to work,' she says coldly.

'Of course.'

'You don't seem to be convinced.'

'You misunderstand me.'

'You're a gentleman. Please be reasonable.'

'I shall love you forever,' I call out after her as she leaves the room.

* * *

Come with me on a strange trip. A terrible day: my brother scolding, my uncle thundering: 'School! School!' *Let us wander in the country lanes, a long strange trip, north and south, night and day. We'll stop at every village for food and drink.* 'I'm over twenty-one!'

* * *

'*I've seen you together.*'[46] I see you together in the passage to the bathroom. It's Dream-Boy Sarhan. He gently pinches your cheek. You do not raise your head in protest. Your charming face is lit by a happy smile. Your plaited hair sways skittishly, the way things do in a cornfield. So the peasant has got in first. That's all right, just as long as we observe absolute equality of opportunity, even if he winds up with two evenings when I get only one.

* * *

Climbing into the Ford, I laugh and laugh. *Ferekeeko*, don't blame me.

*   *   *

I give Tolba Marzuq a lift to the Trianon and he asks me to have a drink with him. Sarhan is there with another man. We exchange a passing nod. When Tolba asks me how I spend my time, I tell him that I drive around making plans for my new business.

'Have you any business experience?'

'No.'

'Then don't throw your money away.'

'But I've made up my mind.'

'You should get yourself a wife. You'd learn to be more cautious with your money.'

I can hardly control my anger. 'I'm determined to stay a bachelor and get on with a project.'

'A smart boy,' he says, indicating Sarhan. 'A friend of mine works at the same firm. They speak of him there as a zealous revolutionary. That's enough, isn't it?'

'Don't you think he's a phoney?'

'We live in a jungle. Beasts of prey are fighting over the loot—our property!' I find a secret satisfaction in listening to him. 'Under those uniforms,' he continues, 'they're mad for luxury.'

'But you can't deny there have been a few reforms?' I am feeling comfortable in our privacy.

His mouth twitches. 'All meant for the diversion of this ignorant mob, who don't have the head for it all. We're at the mercy of the Uniforms.'

Sarhan joins me as I leave the tea-room. I give him a lift to the *pension*. He's a friendly bastard. And though I heartily detest him, I'd rather stay on good terms. He may come in useful some day.

'A fine conquest.' I nudge him with my elbow. He shows a puzzled smile. 'Zohra.' He raises his thick eyebrows in surprise, then lowers them in virtual confession. 'You're an open-handed country boy. Don't grudge me a share.'

'To tell the truth,' he says humourlessly, 'I don't understand you.'

'Let's be frank, just between friends—is it her you pay or Madame?'

'No, no!' he protests. 'It's not the way you think.'

'What way should I think, then?'

'She's a good girl. She's not like that, believe me.'

'All right! Okay! I seem to have mistaken a private vehicle for some form of public transport.'

Don't worry yourself over trifles, *Ferekeeko*!

I've made a mistake, all right. I've taken the New Age for my friend when it's really my enemy. But never mind—I'm happy in my freedom. So what if my class has left me to the waves and the boat sinking? How marvellous to be loyal to nothing, to be free, completely free, free of claims from class, country, or any duty whatever. And all I know of faith is that God is merciful and compassionate. *Ferekeeko*, don't blame me!

*　　*　　*

A terrible commotion, unheard of at a place like the *pension*. Just woken from my siesta, I run out into the hall to see what's happening. A fight in the entry way, which I watch from behind a screen. It's rather entertaining: a strange woman holding our friend Beheiry by the throat, cursing and flailing him, with Zohra standing there nervously, trying to pull them apart. The woman suddenly turns on her, but Zohra is a magnificent fighter and punches her twice, banging the stranger each time into the wall. She's a lovely girl, Zohra, but as tough as an old boot.

I stay behind the screen for a while, the best seat in the house, then when other doors open behind me, I emerge from behind the screen and take the strange woman firmly by the wrist. I pull her gently out, apologizing and trying to calm her down. She is seething with anger, swearing non-stop, and doesn't seem to know I'm there.

Not bad as women go. I stop her when we get to the second floor. 'Wait a bit! You should tidy yourself up before you go out.' She smoothes her hair, takes out a hairpin and pins up a tear on her dress. I give her my handkerchief—it's scented—to wipe her face. 'My car's at the door. I can take you home if you'll let me.'

She looks at me for the first time. I am in my pyjamas and dressing-gown. She thanks me. In the car I ask her where she wants me to take her.

'Mazarita,' she replies in a hoarse voice.

The sky is clouded and it is dark soon, sooner than one would have expected. I try to draw her into conversation.

'You shouldn't get so worked up.'

'The filthy bastard!' she hisses.

'He seems to be a nice country boy.'

She says again, 'Filthy bastard.'

'Your fiancé?' I enjoy my own sarcasm.

She doesn't answer. She is still burning with rage. Really not bad, as women go, and on fire somewhere, that's for sure. We stop in front of a building on Sharia Lido. 'You're a decent man,' she says as she opens the door of the car.

'Are you sure you're all right? I don't want to leave you unless you're recovered.'

'I'm all right, thank you.'

'Then it's goodbye, is it?'

'I work at the Genevoise,' she says, giving me her hand.

I start the car wanting to know more about her. Same old story, I suppose, a runaway boyfriend and the usual fracas. Now that he's met Zohra he's started a new romance. The woman is passable. I may need her some night. But why did I take the trouble to drive her home? Stupid! *Ferekeeko*, don't blame me!

By the time I get back to the *pension* I've forgotten her.

*   *   *

My car eats up the tarmac of crazed streets, lampposts and eucalyptus trees flying past in the opposite direction. Pure speed revives the heart, sweeping boredom away, while the wind howls like a maniac rattling the branches and the leaves of trees, and rain beats down, washing the fields bright green. From Qaitbay to Abu Qir, from the harbour to Siyouf, from the heart to the farthest limbs of the city, wherever there are roads, I wander with my car.

Time has passed and I've taken no serious steps as far as business is concerned. Then it occurs to me to conduct a systematic investigation of certain familiar centres of radiation. I pay a visit to an old procuress at Chatby; she brings me a girl who isn't bad to begin the day with. I have lunch with another madame in the neighbourhood of the Sporting Club, who provides me an Armenian woman somewhat above the average.

And then my Sidi Gaber[47] madame presents me with a lovely piece (Italian mother, Syrian father) whom I insist on taking out in my car. She plays shy a little, says she's worried about the possibility of a storm, but I tell her I wish it would rain, I want it to. All the while I make love to her in the car, she keeps looking at the gathering clouds and saying: 'What if it starts to rain?'

And finally, there on the open country road to Abu Qir, it begins to pour, just as I've been hoping it would. The place is deserted. I shut the windows and watch the deluge, the dancing boughs, the endlessly stretching landscape. The Italo-Syrian beauty at my side is in a panic.

'You're crazy.'

'Just think,' I say, trying to calm her down, 'The two of us, naked in a car, but safe and sound all the same, kissing each other to the clap of thunder and the sound of the driving rain!'

'This is impossible,' she says.

'But just think. Wouldn't you like, from this snug little shelter in the midst of cosmic rage, to stick your tongue out at the entire world?'

'Impossible,' she says. 'Impossible.'

'Yes, but it will happen. Any minute now, my love.' I drink straight from the bottle. And the more the thunder claps the more I ask for, begging the sky to pour down its whole hoard of rain.

'But the car may break down!' says my beauty.

'Amen!'

'It will be dark soon!'

'Let it be dark forever.'

'You're crazy! Crazy!'

'*Ferekeeko*,' I shout into the storm, 'do not blame me!'

*　　*　　*

At breakfast I hear about Zohra's strange new resolution. The *fellaha* wants an education! Many comments, much joking, but everyone is generally encouraging. My old wound gives a twinge. Nobody looked after me when I grew up; I ran wild. I had no regrets then, but I've found out since, too late, that time is no friend. And now here's a *fellaha* who wants to learn to read. Madame explains the girl's situation and why she left her home village, all of which shows that she is not one of Madame's disciples. She may even be a virgin, unless Sarhan the Dream-Boy doesn't care for virgins.

'I thought Zohra was . . .' I say to Madame slyly, with an eloquent gesture.

'No, no,' she assures me.

I change the subject abruptly. 'I wonder if you've thought of any business we could share?'

The cunning old girl asks, 'Where would I get the money?'

'What would happen if occasionally I brought a friend or two here?'

'I'm sorry.' She shakes her head. 'The house is full. And if I let one of you do that, wouldn't I have to let the others too? But you know, I could give you an address if you like.'

When I see Zohra in the hall, I congratulate her on her decision. 'Work hard! I'll soon need a secretary for my business.' She smiles happily, looking very pretty. I still want the girl, even knowing beforehand that I'd be sick of her in a week. It's a week I need, though.

*　　*　　*

I drive round the city. The weather is too mild for my mood. For top speed I go to the desert road, drive for an hour at seventy-five miles an hour, then turn back. I have lunch at the Pam Pam[48] and pick up a girl as she is leaving a hairdresser's.

I go home to the *pension* around dusk. Zohra is sitting in the living-room with a girl I do not know, obviously the teacher. I sit down with Madame, occasionally stealing a look at the teacher. Not bad. Somewhat hunched about the shoulders, but not too noticeably. A little snub nose. Quite attractive, in fact. It's a pity a girl like her won't go in for a quick night of love. It would have to be a lengthy romance and, what's more, she'd probably look forward to wedlock, unpatriotically ignoring the Revolution's call for population control.

Madame introduces me, complete with my hundred *feddans*, business plans and all. I appreciate her tact; she's an old hand. After that I make a point of driving in the direction of her school in Moharrem Bey.[49] It works. I see her one afternoon at a bus stop; I stop the car and invite her in. She hesitates for a moment, but the sky is cloudy and threatening. All the way home I complain of loneliness in Alexandria. I need someone to consult on my business . . .

'I do think we should meet again,' I say at the door.

'Drop in by all means. My father would be delighted to meet you.'

Now, *Ferekeeko*, the truth is, I am quite an eligible match, young and rich. If I want to be safe in the company of these college girls I'll have to wear a fake wedding ring!

That evening I have nothing to do. I drop in on the Maltese madame at Cleopatra and ask her to call in as many of her girls as she can. I have a wonderful time—a wild evening, studded with delightful follies unheard of since the days of our great Haroun el-Rasheed.

*　　*　　*

'I can't be hard on him. He never saw his mother. His father died when he was six.' He was speaking calmly, but my brother was trembling with rage.

*　　*　　*

I am holed up with skeletons. I hate old Qalawoon. The day I see his face in the morning is always a bad day. Tolba Marzuq asks about the progress of my plans. I catch a whiff of incense in the hall and look interrogatively at him.

'It's Madame. You should have seen her make the round of the rooms with the incense-burner.'

'So you like Umm Kulthum and use incense to keep off the evil eye. Very Egyptian for a Greek.' Mine hostess gives me a fleeting smile. She is absorbed in listening to a Greek song on the radio. 'I'm looking for some foreigner who'd be ready to sell out. So many of them are leaving just now.'

'A good idea. What do you think, Mariana?'

'Yes. Wait a moment! I think the proprietor of the Miramar Café means to sell out.' She speaks quickly, turning back to the song.

'What does it say?'

'It's about a young girl. She is describing to her mother the sort of man she'd like to marry.' Her old face grimaces coyly. I look at the Captain's portrait and her ancient photograph. 'I could have been a lady to this day.'

'You are. A perfect lady.'

'I mean lady of the big house in Ibrahimiya.'

'You mustn't waste your time,' says the Doddering Caliph. 'Take up some business.'

I curse him under my breath.

It is bitterly cold outside and I have a date with my Italo-Syrian beauty at the madame's house in Sidi Gaber. *Ferekeeko,* don't blame me!

*　　*　　*

53

At breakfast I hear that Zohra's sister and her brother-in-law have paid a stormy visit to the *pension.*

'She has made up her mind to stay here for good.' Madame says that with deep satisfaction. 'Thank god they didn't strangle her!'

'Apparently you Beheirys are weaklings,' I say to Sarhan.

'What do you mean, weaklings?'

'The close proximity of your province to Alexandria has obviously weakened its native traditions.'

'We are more civilized than other provinces. That's all.'

*　　*　　*

I give Tolba Marzuq a lift to the Windsor Hotel, where he is to meet an old friend. I like the old man and respect him deeply. To me he is the image of a venerable monarch who has been dethroned, but still keeps his personal dignity. I joke.

'Don't you think the *fellaha* should have gone home with her people?'

'She shouldn't have run away in the first place.'

'I mean she must have had some strong reason for not going back, even if she wished to.'

'You mean the Beheiry lad?'

'Not particularly, though I'm sure he's partly responsible.'

'Who knows?' He smiles. 'He may be innocent after all. Maybe when she ran away from home it was some other fellow.'

The news that she has rejected Mahmoud Abu el Abbas adds to my wonder. Before applying to Madame for the hand of her maid, the fellow had consulted me.

I stop at his stall the next day knowing that he will open the subject. We exchange significant looks.

'That's modern girls for you!'

'The fool! She won't get another offer in a hurry.'

'You'll marry a better girl some day. Actually, I don't believe the *pension* is a very suitable place for getting yourself a wife.'

'I thought she was decent and well-behaved.'

'I haven't said anything to the contrary, but . . .'

'Yes?'

'Why should you care, now that you're through with it all?'

'I have to find out why she turned me down.'

'She's in love with Sarhan el-Beheiry. If that's any help to you.'

'The idiot! Would Mr. Sarhan marry her?'

'I said love. Not marriage.'

I've detested this Dream-Boy from the start. My dislike has sometimes been overcome by his friendliness, but only momentarily. All this has nothing to do with Zohra; she's not that important. Maybe it's his bumbling tactlessness that annoys me so much. Or is it just that way he has of singing the glory of the Revolution on every possible occasion? I have to hold my tongue, unwillingly acquiescing in these hymns of praise, but one day I burst out: 'All right, we all believe in the Revolution, but the past wasn't a total blank!'

'Yes, it was,' he insists.

'The Corniche was there, and so was the University of Alexandria.'

'The Corniche wasn't for the people, nor was the University. Why should you have a hundred *feddans* of your own,' he asks with a smile, without malice, 'when my whole family holds only ten?'

'Why should you have ten, when millions of peasants haven't even got a job?'

* * *

I won't believe a word of what you say. You're just mad because Mervat turned you down. And you don't believe any of this rubbish about socialism and equality. It's simply power. If you have power you have everything. And meanwhile there's no harm in preaching socialism and equality to others. Have you actually seen any of that gang walking around in poverty lately, like our lord Omar?[50]

* * *

A little while later I get wind of a lovely fight between the newsboy Mahmoud Abu el Abbas and Sarhan el-Beheiry, our hero from onion country. He says nothing about it, however, and I respect his silence. When we are alone in the living-room one evening I even consult him on my plans.

'Don't take up that café business,' he urges. 'You're a man of good family, you must think of something more suitable.'

'Such as?'

'Now that I think of it, well, why not a poultry and dairy farm? There's a lot of money in that. We could rent a plot of land in

Semouha. I have experience, friends. I might even come in as a partner, if I could get the capital.'

*   *   *

Alexandria. How small it becomes when you look at it from behind the wheel of my madcap motorcar. I can cut through it like the wind but it keeps turning itself, in spite of me, into a tin of sardines. Night follows day in dogged stupidity, nothing ever happens. Dawn after dawn the sky gets up and dresses itself, the weather does its usual tricks, and the women arrive in all colours, shapes and sizes. But nothing ever happens. The universe is really dead, you know. These are only the ultimate twitches before rigor mortis sets in.

I remember the Genevoise. One facade to the Corniche, bravely defying the sea and the season, but the actual entrance is through a narrow side street. Inside there's a stage at one end of the hall and a dance-floor in the middle. The walls, ceiling and lamps are a dirty red—a jinn's hide-out—and one look at the girls and the clientele is enough to tell you the place is a brothel.

Beheiry's girl is performing an authentic belly-dance, with a fair amount of obscenity. I ask her to my table. At first she doesn't recognize me, then she apologizes for her conduct the day we met and explains that after such a lapse of time she'd stopped expecting me. She says her name is Safeya Barakat. God knows what her real name is. She is, in fact, better looking than the teacher; a little fat, though, and there's a distinctly professional look about her plump face.

I drink so much that I almost pass out. I invite her into my car and take her to Sharia Lido in Mazarita. On the way I try to make love but she says she's sorry, she has the curse. I go back to the *pension* in a deplorable condition, deeply disappointed. Zohra is just leaving the bathroom in her shift. I block her way with open arms.

'Go away,' she says firmly.

I beckon her to my room.

'Leave me alone!' She threatens me.

Excited with drink and desire, I throw myself at her. She fights me off, beating my chest with her fists so fiercely that I'm enraged and go berserk. I start hitting her savagely, determined to shove her or drag her into my room. Then I feel a hand on my shoulder and hear Sarhan. He is breathing hard.

'Hosny, have you gone mad?'

I push him away firmly, but his grip on my shoulder tightens.

'Go into the bathroom,' he says, 'And stick a finger down your throat. You'll feel better if you get it out of your system.'

I turn on him suddenly and hit him in the face. He reels, then hits back in a rage. Then Madame comes in, pulling on her dressing-gown.

'What's the matter?' she asks anxiously, her voice rising. 'No, no, gentlemen, you'll wreck the place! I won't stand for it! I won't stand for it!' She says the words furiously, breaking us apart.

*　　*　　*

Cherubs float or dance on the ceiling. Rain beats on the window and the waves make a deafening barrage. I close my eyes; my head aches badly. I yawn and I curse everything. I curse as I realize that I have slept in my coat and shoes. I curse again as the events of the awful night come back to me in a rush.

Madame enters and stands looking down at me as I try lethargically to get up. 'You're late,' she says reproachfully, taking the big chair. 'You shouldn't drink so much.' Our eyes meet and she smiles. 'You're my favourite lodger, but please don't drink so much.'

'I'm sorry,' I say after a while, staring at the cherubs overhead. 'I should apologize to Zohra.'

'Good! But promise you'll conduct yourself as a gentleman of your family should.'

'Give her my apology, then.'

After that I cut Sarhan completely, though I manage with some difficulty to conciliate Zohra. But I must admit that I miss Sarhan's company. The other fellow, Mansour Bahy, I hardly know. We usually exchange bare civilities at breakfast and then settle back to loathe each other cordially in silence. I can't help despising him, with his arrogant effeminate introversion and his vulgar, acquired *politesse*. What a shock his voice on the radio gives me now. You'd think it was the voice of a fine orator, a hero. What a fraud. Curious. No one at the *pension* likes him except the Doddering Sultan. The old man must be an ex-pervert.

*　　*　　*

Maybe I shouldn't leave the room, but some sort of auspicious event is taking place outside. Could it be in Beheiry's room? Yes. A little disagreement? A quarrel, a fight in fact, between the Beheiry Romeo and the Beheiry Juliet. What can it be? Has she submitted a request that he repair his technical oversight and make her an honest woman? And is he shirking the responsibility, as he did with Safeya? Delicious! I'd better stay in. I never thought there was so much entertainment in store for me in this place. Listen carefully, *Ferekeeko*, and enjoy it all.

'It's none of your business! Yes, I'll marry anyone I like! I'll marry Aleya!'

Ya Sayyid! Ya Badawi! Aleya! The schoolmistress! Has Dream-Boy accepted that standing invitation she offers everyone to visit her *en famille*? So he's switched his affections from the scholar to the teacher! *Ferekeeko*, be my witness! Long live the Revolution! Long live the July Ordinances![51] Alexandria, what a lovely day!

Here is Madame's voice, remonstrating in pidgin Arabic; and the great newscaster himself in the flesh, having condescended to interest himself in the affairs of the commonalty. He's sure to find a solution to this rustic imbroglio. *A moi!* Welcome the fray! Action, *Ferekeeko*! Never let events forestall you.

I hear the story later from mine hostess. 'I have given him notice to leave,' she says angrily. 'I shouldn't have accepted him in the first place.'

I praise her protective attitude towards Zohra and enquire after the girl.

'She's not well. She keeps to her room.'

'The old story. It keeps coming round like the four seasons of the year. The Beheiry must be glad to leave. He's been promoted to the fifth floor. Who knows where his extraordinary talents will take him from there?'

'The proprietor downstairs is thinking seriously of selling the Miramar Café,' Madame ventures.

'I am ready to talk,' I say with aplomb.

I go out with every intention of painting the town red. *Ferekeeko*, don't blame me.

*   *   *

She is deathly pale, with a new look of defeat about her, the light gone from her hazel eyes. She pours my tea and makes for the

58

door, but I beg her to stay. The wind is blowing outside and clouds are gathering. The room suddenly darkens.

'Zohra, you always have to take the good with the bad. The world's full of wicked people. But there's still a lot of kindness in it.' She isn't listening. She doesn't seem to care about anything. 'Take me, for instance. I was fed up with life at home. That's why I'm here.' Not a word. She isn't interested. 'I tell you, nothing lasts forever, neither sorrow nor joy. We have to go on living. When hard luck leads us down a closed path, we have to look for another. That's all.'

'Everything's all right. I regret nothing.'

'But Zohra, you're sad, miserable. You have every reason to be. But you must find a way out. You've got to.' She can hardly control herself. Her face, distorted with grief, looks ugly for a second. 'Listen to me, I've something to tell you. Think it over, take your time. I'll be going into business soon—and I'll give you a good job.' She doesn't seem to trust me. 'This place is hopeless. A girl like you and a pack of wolves!' It's obvious that she doesn't take a word of what I'm saying seriously. 'You'll be safe with me. A good job and a fine life.'

She mumbles something I can't hear, takes the tray and leaves the room.

I lose my temper, angry at her and at myself to the point of loathing. Being able to play upon the starved passions of frustrated men appears to have blinded mademoiselle to her own true value—curse the land that gave you birth! And sourly I say: '*Ferekeeko!* Don't put the blame on me!'

* * *

I spend an evening within the dingy red walls of the Genevoise, guzzling with Safeya, and later she takes me home to her flat, where I pour my drunken troubles into her ears. When I mention my plan for buying a business, she sits up.

'There's a wonderful opening for you!' She lights a cigarette and speaks more deliberately. 'The Genevoise. The owner wants to sell out.'

'But it's seedy. And depressing.'

'Think of the situation: on the Corniche, near the centre of town. It will make a marvellous restaurant and nightclub. It brings in good money even now, and it's sure to bring in more once we've done it over.' She goes on: 'Look, you're a man of family.

The police won't meddle with you in a hurry. And I've got masses of experience in this sort of business. The summer season's a sure thing and so's the rest of the year, thanks to the Libyans. Petrodollars!'

'All right. Arrange a meeting with the boss.' It's as if I'm in a trance.

'Good! And I'll be responsible for the female staff. Now,' she suggests, kissing me, 'why don't you come and live here with me?'

'Why not? But you've got to have one thing clear if we mean to get along together. I don't believe in love. I don't even know what it is.'

*　　*　　*

I get back to the *pension* at about ten o'clock in the morning and in the porter's hall I run into Sarhan. We ignore each other, waiting for the lift without a word. Is he paying a visit, I wonder, to his future in-laws? Suddenly he speaks to me:

'I know very well you were behind the trouble with Mahmoud Abu el Abbas.' I turn a cold shoulder, deliberately cutting him. 'He told me,' he goes on. 'Anyway, it was a rotten thing for you to do.'

He is getting excited and I'm furious already.

'Shut up, you son of a bitch!'

We close, slugging each other until the porters separate us.

'I'll teach you something,' he shouts, 'you just wait!'

'Come on then. It would give me a big kick to relieve you of your dirty rotten life.'

*　　*　　*

It's early evening and Madame and Tolba Bey are sitting in the living-room listening to the radio.

'Come on,' says the lady, 'give us your advice. Where shall we spend New Year's Eve? *He* thinks we should go to the Monseigneur. But Amer Bey says we should stay at home.'

'Where is Amer Bey?'

'In bed, with a cold.'

'Then let him stay in bed and let's go to the Monseigneur. We'll have a really good time drinking till morning.'

I tell her later, 'You know, I've found it at last.'

'What?'

'The business investment I've been looking for.'

She is obviously disappointed at the news. 'Don't be in too much of a hurry,' she advises. 'You must think it over.'

'I've had enough of thinking.'

'The Miramar Café is a better investment.' She hesitates. 'And I was thinking seriously of coming in as a partner.'

'I may have plans later to expand the business.' I grin, suddenly possessed by the desire to enjoy my New Year's Eve to the full.

I go to see the proprietor of the Genevoise in his office, where we agree as to preliminaries. He invites me to come to his house in Camp de César[52] after closing time. Safeya is there to take part in discussing the details, and they both suggest that I spend New Year's Eve at the Genevoise: we can come back later to the Frenchman's house or go somewhere else. In any case I'm delighted at the idea of being rid of the old people's party.

*   *   *

I meet strange looks at breakfast. Madame and Tolba Bey have something queer about their faces. Old Qalawoon is keeping to his room, so is Mansour Bahy, and there's no sign of Zohra. My table-companions are silent, but their expressions suggest something ominous.

'Have you heard the news?' Tolba finally blurts out. 'Sarhan el-Beheiry was found dead last night. On the deserted road that goes to the Palma.'

'Dead?'

'Murdered, perhaps!'

'But . . .'

'Here's the paper,' Madame interrupts. 'It's terrible. I think there'll be trouble.'

I remember our fighting in the porter's hall and am seized with depression. Will I get into trouble? I say stupidly: 'I wonder who did it?'

'That is the question,' says Madame.

'I suppose they'll make enquiries about his enemies,' one of the old men says.

'Among us, as it so happens,' I observe ironically, 'he certainly had no friends.'

'He may have had other enemies.'

'Sooner or later they'll find out the truth. God's will be done!' I feel barely recovered from the impact of the news. Then I ask about Zohra.

'She's in her room,' says Madame. 'In terrible shape.'

I'd meant to give Madame notice of my leaving but decide to postpone it for the moment. When he sees that I'm on the point of going out, Tolba warns me:

'We'll probably be summoned for the investigation.'

'I'll be there all right,' I say at the door. 'Let them call us.'

I ought to clear my head, with a wild drive from one end of Alexandria to the other. *White clouds sail slowly above my head, almost within reach, drenched with colours; the air is light and sharp.* This is the last day of the old year and my lust for a hectic roaring time goes up a thousand per cent. Let them live or die, who cares? I know what I'm going to do. And as I put my car in gear, I tell my reflection in the mirror: *'Ferekeeko,* don't blame me.'

3. MANSOUR BAHY

'So I'm to stay prisoner here in Alexandria, to spend the rest of my life trying to justify myself.' With that I said goodbye to my brother and went straight to the Pension Miramar. The judas opened, showing the face of an old woman, fine-featured in spite of her age.

'Madame Mariana?'

'Yes?'

'I'm Mansour Bahy.'

She opened the door wide. 'Welcome. Your brother spoke to me on the phone. Make yourself at home.'

We waited at the door for the porter to bring up my two suitcases. She invited me to take a seat and sat down herself under a statue of the Madonna.

'Your brother is a very distinguished police officer indeed. He used to stay here occasionally before his marriage. Before he was transferred to Cairo. After working here for so many years!' She is very friendly, but examines me closely all the same. 'You live with your brother?'

'Yes.'

'Are you a student?'

'No. I work at the Alexandria Broadcasting Service.'

'But you come from Cairo, originally?'

'Yes, I do.'

'Well, make yourself at home and don't mention the rent.'

I laughed incredulously, but I'd already guessed she would give me a room for nothing, if I wished. Marvellous. The rank breath of corruption everywhere. But who am I to throw stones?

'How long will you stay?'

'Indefinitely.'

'Good. You'll pay a moderate rent and I won't raise it in summer.'

'Thank you, but my brother let me know what I ought to do. In summer I shall pay at the summer rate.'

She tactfully changed the subject. 'You're not married, are you?'

'No.'

'When do you think you might get married?'

'I haven't thought about it yet. Not now anyway.'

'What do you think about then?'

She laughed. So did I, without wanting to.

The doorbell rang and a girl came in with a big parcel of groceries. Very attractive. The housemaid, obviously. Madame spoke to her. Zohra. She was the same age as my friends at the University and that was where she should have been, not running errands for the old lady.

Madame showed me two rooms overlooking the sea-front. 'This side is not very suitable for winter,' she murmured apologetically, 'but all the other rooms are taken.'

'I like winter,' I answered casually.

I stood alone on the balcony. The sea lay there under me, a beautiful clear aquamarine, little wavelets sparkling in the sun; a light cool wind caressed my face and there were a few white clouds in the sky. I felt almost overwhelmed with melancholy.

Then I heard someone move behind me in the room. It was Zohra, making up the bed with fresh sheets, intent on her work, not looking in my direction. I watched her carefully, and was soon aware of her *fellaha* beauty. 'Thank you, Zohra.' My tone was sociable, and she gave me a pleasant smile. I asked her for a cup of coffee, which she came back with in a few minutes. 'Wait until I finish, please.' I put the saucer on the parapet and sipped my coffee while she stood waiting on the threshold, looking absently at the sea. 'Do you like nature?' She didn't answer, as if she didn't understand my question. I wondered what she thought about. As the daughter of this good earth, I thought, her instincts are probably vibrating for the prime creative act of nature.

'I have a lot of books in this trunk,' I said, trying to make conversation. 'And there's no bookcase in this room.'

She looked round at the pieces of furniture. 'Keep them in the trunk?'

I smiled at her simplicity. 'Have you been here long?'

'No.'

'You . . . like the place?'

'Yes.'

'Don't the men annoy you?'

She shrugged.

'They can be quite dangerous, you know.'

She took away the cup. As she finally left the room, she said, 'I'm not scared.' I admired her self-assurance.

Then I went back to my own sense of frustration, my habitual thoughts, brooding on how things are, how they should be, drifting into my usual depression.

I examined the furniture again. I'll have to buy a little bookcase, I thought, but the little table standing between the wardrobe and the chaise-longue would do for writing.

* * *

I worked for some hours at the Studio recording my weekly programme, had lunch at Petro's in Sharia Safeya Zaghloul, then went to Ala Keifak in Ramleh Square for my coffee, where I sat watching the square, busy under an overcast sky.

Raincoats were at the ready and people were hurrying by. All at once my heart gave a thump. That man there—Fawzi! I leaned forward, my forehead touching the window. Was it Fawzi? No. Of course not, not Fawzi, just a very close resemblance. (And then Doreya came to mind—by the law of association, as they say. Though she was always there, in fact, by her own law. Yes. Doreya.) But supposing it were Fawzi and our eyes met? Old friends would naturally have to greet each other with open arms. He was my mentor, after all, my professor. Then let me embrace him fervently, in spite of the thorns. He's seen me. Here he comes.

I asked him to sit down to a cup of coffee. Politeness demanded no less.

'I'm delighted to see you. What brings you to Alexandria at this time of the year?'

'A family visit.'

Which meant that he was here on Party business,[53] but was keeping the fact from me—as he should.

'Well, I hope you have a pleasant stay.'

'It's been two years since we saw you last. Not since you graduated, in fact.'

'Yes. You know I was posted to Alexandria.'

'I mean that you seem to have deserted us completely.'

'I had some troubles.'

'Perhaps it was wise to quit working for a cause so uncongenial to you.'

'And perhaps it's wise to stop working for a cause you no longer have any faith in.' I retorted, blindly, defensively, full of pride.

He paused, weighing his words as he always did. 'They say your brother ...'

'I'm over twenty-one,' I said irritably.

'I'm sorry. I've annoyed you, have I?' He laughed.

My nerves were on edge. (Doreya!) A light shower began and I wished it would come down in torrents, clearing the square and leaving it deserted. (My love, don't believe them! Some old sage once said that in order to convince each other of the truth we may sometimes have to tell lies.) I looked at my dangerous friend.

'Don't you care about anything at all?' he asked me.

I almost laughed out loud. 'As long as I'm alive, I must care about something.'

'Such as?'

'Can't you see that I've shaved and arranged my tie neatly?'

'And what else?' he said gravely.

'Have you seen the new film at the Metro?'

'Good idea. Let's go and see a capitalist film!'

*   *   *

Madame paid a courtesy visit to my room. 'Is there anything you need? Anything I can do for you? *Do* tell me! Your brother was always very frank with me. And so gallant—a real friend in need! And so big! A giant—but you're so finely built yourself—and strong, too! Consider the Pension Miramar your home. Think of me as a friend, a real friend in every sense of the word.'

It wasn't courtesy that brought her, but the chance to fulfil herself in an orgy of verbal self-expression. She gave me her life story: her early well-to-do youth, her first love and marriage to an English captain, her second marriage to the Caviare King, the big house at Ibrahimiya, the comedown. Not an ordinary comedown, though: hers was the Pension of Quality, of the Pashas and Beys, of the good old days of World War Two.

She invited me to tell her in exchange everything about myself. She gushed questions—a strange, tiresome, entertaining woman, a fading female. But even though I was seeing her only as an old ruin clinging to the rag-ends of life, it was still quite possible to

66

imagine her—I could picture it all in the light of the old stories of autocrats and famous beauties—as the queen of brilliant *salons*.

At breakfast I was introduced to the other guests. What a weird assortment! But I needed a pastime, and if I could get the better of my introversion, I thought, I could find some companionship here. Why not? But let's not even think about Amer Wagdi and Tolba Marzuq; they belong to a dying generation. Then, I wondered, what about Sarhan or Hosny? In Sarhan's eyes there was a native compatibility. He seemed sympathetic, in spite of his awful voice. But what were his interests? By contrast, Hosny simply got on my nerves—that at least was my first impression of him. He was arrogantly taciturn and reserved and I didn't like his massive build, his big haughty head or the way he sat enthroned, sprawling in his chair like a lord, but a lord without any real sovereignty or substance. I presumed he'd feel at conversational ease only with someone he knew to be even more stupid and trifling than himself. He who deserts his monastery, I reminded myself, must be content with the company of the profane. And as usual my introversion got the better of me: They will say . . . They will think . . .

Reasoning like that had once made me lose the chance of a lifetime.

*   *   *

I was surprised one morning to see Sarhan el-Beheiry come into my office at the studio. Beaming like an old friend, he shook my hand warmly.

'Just passing by. I thought I'd drop in to see you and have a cup of coffee with you.' I said he was welcome, of course, and ordered the coffee. 'Some day I'll want to pick your brain about the secrets of broadcasting.'

With pleasure, I thought, you past master at loafing[54] I've never had the luck to be able to enjoy. He talked about his work at the Alexandria Mills, his membership in its board of directors and its ASU Base Unit.[55]

'How wonderfully active you are! You're a splendid example to the uncommitted.'

He gave me a long searching look. 'It's our path towards building a New World.'

'Did you believe in socialism before the Revolution?'

'Actually, my conviction was born with the Revolution.'

I was aching to query this conviction of his, but thought the better of it. We were soon discussing the *pension*.

'A most interesting group,' he said. 'One never gets enough of their company.'

'What about Hosny Allam?' I asked cautiously.

'A nice chap, too.'

'He seems like the Sphinx to me.'

'Not really. He's a nice chap. He's got a natural talent for pleasure.' We smiled at each other. Unwittingly he had given me the key to his own character rather than to Allam's. 'He's a man of property, with no fixed profession. He probably has no degree. Remember that,' he cautioned. 'He has a hundred *feddans*, so he's entrenched in the front lines of the old regime. And without a degree. I suppose you can guess the rest.'

'Why does he live in Alexandria?'

'He knows what's what. He's looking for some business.'

'He'd better wipe that arrogant look off his face or he'll frighten away his customers.'

I asked Sarhan why he lived in a *pension* even though he had been so long in Alexandria. He answered, but not spontaneously.

'I preferred a busy guest-house to a flat on my own in town.'

*   *   *

The evening of the Umm Kulthum concert, an evening of drinking and music, during which many a hidden soul was bared. Naturally it was Sarhan el-Beheiry, who probably contributed least to the expense, who was mainly responsible for bringing us together.

I stole a few looks at Tolba Marzuq. No one guessed what he meant to me: old recollections, dreams of bloodshed, of classes in conflict, books and pamphlets studied in secret meetings, a whole edifice of ideas. I was appalled at his flabbiness and humility, the compulsive movements of his cheeks, his abject cowering in his seat, his hypocritical playing up to the Revolution, as if he were not descended from men who had amassed their power from the flesh and blood of the people. It was his turn to play the flattering fool, now that his withered glory had left us with a nation of parasites. And Hosny is just a wing of this broken eagle, I thought, which still flutters with life, and may manage at any moment to limp into some grotesque sort of flight.

'*I tell you all the old class barriers have been wiped out.*'

'*No. They've only given place to other ones. You'll see.*'

Sarhan was the soul of the group, infusing us with constant hilarity. He was kind-hearted, candid. Why not? Ambitious, to be sure, since his was basically an opportunist's interpretation of the Revolution.

Of them all, however, I soon found that Amer Wagdi was the most fascinating and the most worthy of affection and esteem. He was the Amer Wagdi whose articles I had reread for my radio programme; 'Generations of Revolutionaries'. I had been taken by his progressive but contradictory ideas and charmed by his style, which had developed from conventional rhyming prose[56] into a relatively simple but powerful idiom charged with occasional grandeur. My recognizing him and his writings pleased him so much that I could sense how injured he felt by callous neglect. It touched me deeply. He seized the opportunity like a drowning man clutching at a straw and gave me the story of his life, his long fight for the Nationalist cause, the political waves he had struggled against, the great heroes in whom he had believed.

'And what about Saad Zaghloul? The older generation worshipped him.'

'What good are such idols? He stabbed the true workers' revolution to death at its birth.'

Why did Tolba Marzuq give me such furtive looks? I caught his eye in the mirror of the hat-stand, suspicious, hostile. I poured him a drink and asked his opinion of Amer Wagdi's glimpses of history.

'Thank you,' he said, as if to excuse himself. 'Let bygones be bygones. Let's listen to the music.'

Zohra served us admirably, but she rarely smiled at our jokes. When she sat next to the folding screen she watched us at a distance, her limpid eyes saying nothing. She was serving Hosny Allam when he asked, 'And you, Zohra, how do you like the Revolution?'

She blushed and turned away from our boisterousness, while Madame answered for her at length. But Hosny had apparently wanted to draw her into the conversation; I could see that he was annoyed by Madam's interruption. 'She likes it instinctively,' I told him. He didn't seem to hear me, though, or perhaps he just ignored me, the pig. Before the end of the concert he disappeared and Zohra said he'd gone out.

I really admired Amer Wagdi, sitting up so late, and thoroughly enjoying the singing and the music. It was almost dawn when we got up to go to bed.

'Was there ever in your day a voice like Umm Kulthum's?'

'No.' He smiled. 'It's the only thing today for which the past can provide no equal.'

* * *

I asked her to sit down, but she just stood there leaning against the wardrobe and gazing with me out through the window at a cloud-laden horizon. She was waiting for me to finish my cup of tea. I usually gave her a biscuit or a piece of cake from a small store I kept in my room, which she accepted in token of a growing friendship. I was pleased that her innocence made her sensitive to the admiration and respect I felt for her.

It began to rain. The small drops streamed down the window-panes, transforming the world outside. I asked her about her village and she chatted with me. I guessed why she was driven from home, but said lightly, 'If you'd stayed at home, you'd have been married by now.'

Then she told me a terrible story about her grandfather and the old man they would have forced her to marry. She concluded, 'And so I ran away.'

I was disturbed. 'But what will people say?'

'I don't care anyway. It's better than what I escaped from.'

My admiration for her grew. But I pitied her for her loneliness, even though she stood there full of self-confidence. Rain stippled the windowpanes with water and mist, making the world almost disappear.

* * *

What was it? A bomb? A rocket? A flash of insanity? No, just a car, with that idiot Hosny Allam at the wheel. What made him drive so insanely? Only he knew. But there was a girl with him. (Looks like Sonya. Is it Sonya?) Oh well, Sonya or not, the hell with him.

A little later I sat at my desk. Then one of my office colleagues came up to me. 'Your friends were arrested yesterday,' he whispered. I was stunned for a minute and couldn't say anything in reply. 'They say it's because . . .'

I cut him short. 'That's not important.'

'There are rumours . . .'

'I said it's not important.'

He leant on my desk. 'Your brother was wise.'

'Yes, very wise.' I sighed with exasperation. Hosny Allam must be at the end of the world by now, I thought, and Sonya must be trembling with fear and desire.

* * *

'Not another word from you! I'm getting you out of this hole.'
'I'm not a child any more.'
'You sent your mother to her grave.'
'I thought we'd agreed not to rake up the past.'
'But I see it in the present. You'll come with me to Alexandria even if I have to carry you there by force.'
'I beg your pardon! You forget I'm a grown man.'
'You're a fool. Did you think we didn't know? We know everything.' He looked hard at me. *'You conceited idiot! What do you take them for? Heroes?'* He grunted. *'I know them better than you do. You're coming with me, whether you like it or not.'*

* * *

She opened the door herself. My heart was hammering; my mouth had gone dry and my head was in a daze. In the dark corridor her face shone white and pale. She stared at me stonily, without recognition. Then her eyes widened in surprise.

She whispered, 'Mr. Mansour.'

She stood aside and I went in.

'How are you, Doreya?'

She led the way to the sitting-room, where everything around her seemed to reflect her own profound unhappiness. We both sat down. His portrait faced us from the opposite wall, looking out at us from a black frame. He was holding a camera, which he seemed to aim at the two of us together. We looked at each other.

'When did you come back?'

'I came straight from the station.'

'You heard . . .?'

'Yes, at the office. I took the two o'clock train.' I looked at his photograph. The smell of his tobacco still hung about the room. 'Did they get them all?'

'I think so.'

'Where did they take them?'

'I've no idea.' Her hair was untidy and her face was pale. She looked wilted, heavy-eyed from anxiety.

'And you?'

'As you see.'

The fact that she was on her own, with no money or resources—he'd been an associate professor of economics, but had no savings—was all too clear.

'Doreya, you're an old friend, and so is he. My best friend . . . in spite of everything.' I gathered my courage and went on. 'I have a good job and income. And I have no one to support, you know.'

She shook her head. 'But you know I can't . . .'

I wouldn't let her go on. 'I didn't think you'd refuse a little help from an old friend.'

'I'll find a job.'

'Yes, all right, but that will take time.'

Nothing had changed in the room. His room, as I'd always known it in the past: the big studio sofa and the bookshelves laden with books, the tape-recorder, the record-player, the television set and the radio, the camera and the film equipment, the albums. (Where's the photograph we had taken at the Auberge in Fayoum?[57] He must have smashed it in a moment of anger.) My eyes met hers, then we both looked away, thinking the same thoughts, touched by the same memories. Past, present and future seemed to meet in a dark road, fearful and unknown.

'Have you any plans?'

'I haven't had time to think.'

'You didn't think of writing to me.'

'No.'

'But it must have occurred to you I might turn up.'

No reply. She left the room and came back with the tea tray. I lighted her cigarette and we sat smoking in silence, while an old unrecollected aroma came stealing back to me. And at last what had to be said was said.

'I suppose you know that I tried to come back and couldn't?' She made no comment. 'I didn't get much encouragement, to put it mildly.'

She murmured, 'Let's forget it. Please.'

'Even Fawzi would have nothing to do with me.'

'I said forget it.'

'Doreya, I know what they said. That I wanted to come back to spy for my brother.'

She pleaded. 'Can't you leave it alone? Can't you see I'm unhappy enough as I am?'

I looked down. 'You know exactly how I feel.'

'I'm very grateful.'

I felt stung. 'I mean the feeling I have that I should have been with them!'

She said sadly, 'It's no good your torturing yourself.'

'I wish—I wish you'd tell me frankly what you think of me.'

'I've received you here in my house—*his* house, if you like.' She spoke in a low voice, after a tense silence. 'That's enough, I should think.'

I sighed with relief, though I wasn't fully reassured: I knew I'd be right back in the old hell. But it was no time for explanations.

'I'll come to see you occasionally. And please write to me if ever you need help.'

* * *

I was very fatigued from travelling, so I stayed in the *pension* and joined the group around the radio. Luckily they were my favourites, Amer Wagdi, Madame, and Zohra. I was preoccupied with my own thoughts, not listening to their conversation, until I heard Madame addressing me.

'You always seem so far away from us all.'

'The intelligent ones are always like that,' said Amer Wagdi, looking at me gently. 'Have you ever thought of bringing out some of the material of your programmes in book form?'

'I'm thinking of writing a programme,' I threw out carelessly, 'about the history of betrayal in Egypt.'

'Betrayal!' The old man laughed. 'What an enormous subject. You must come to me. I'll help you. I'll give you all the necessary references and recollections.'

'I love you. You love me. Why don't you let me talk to him?'

'You're out of your mind.'

'He's a rational man. He'll understand and he'll forgive.'

'Can't you see? He loves me and he considers you his best friend.'

'But he hates falsehood. I understand him perfectly.'

'A programme on betrayal—what a programme that would be! But mind you, write a book in the end or you'll soon be forgotten, as I've been. The only man who survived without writing down his thoughts was Socrates.'

Madame was listening to a Greek song that she herself had requested on the radio. About a virgin listing the qualities of the man of her dreams, or so she says. The sight of her as she listened silently, with her eyes closed, was touching, a tragi-comic image of the irrepressible desire to live.

'It was Plato, a disciple, who gave him immortality,' Amer Wagdi went on. 'But isn't it strange that he should have chosen the poisoned cup when he had the chance to escape?'

'Yes.' I added bitterly, 'And to do so even though he had no sense of guilt.'

'And yet how numerous are the people now who in comparison with Socrates don't even seem to belong to the same species!'

My bitterness bordered on insanity. 'They're betrayers. All of them.'

'There are facts and there are legends. Life is an enigma, my boy.'

'But your generation believed. You had faith.'

'Faith. Doubt.' He chuckled. 'They are like day and night.'

'May I ask what you mean?'

'I mean that they are inseparable.' After a moment of silence, he said, 'And what is your generation like, my boy?'

'What counts is what you do, not what you think,' I answered impatiently. 'And therefore I'm really no more than an idea.'

'Do? Think? What's all this about?' Madame smiled in bemusement.

The old man smiled too. 'Sometimes a tired thinker may come to the conclusion that the best things in the world are a good meal and a pretty woman.'

Madame crowed, 'Bravo! Bravo!'

Zohra laughed. It did me good to hear her laugh for the first time. Then there was a moment of silence, during which we listened to the wind howling outside, driving at the walls and the closed windows.

I felt myself lapsing into anxious depression. 'I'm sure the ideal is to believe and put your beliefs in action. To have nothing to believe in is to be lost forever. But to believe in something and none the less sit there paralysed is sheer hell.'

'I agree. You should have seen Saad Zaghloul in his old age, defying banishment and death.'

I looked at Zohra, the lonely exile. She sat there full of hope and self-confidence. I envied her.

*   *   *

74

The following week I paid Doreya another visit. The place looked as neat and well kept as in the old days and she seemed to be taking care of herself, but of course she was still alone—without hope and without an occupation to fill her time.

'I hope my visits don't disturb you.'

'At least they make me feel that I'm still alive.'

Her voice was lifeless. It almost broke my heart, for it made me imagine the barrenness and poverty of her existence. I longed to be able to tell her something of what I felt, but memories silenced me. We agreed that she should get a job. But how? Her having only a B.A. in classics didn't make it easy.

'Don't shut yourself up in this house.'

'I have thought of that, but I've made no move yet.'

'If I could only see you every day.'

She smiled. 'It would be better,' she said, after thinking a moment, 'if we could meet away from here.'

I was not very happy at the idea, but I could see that she was right. So I agreed.

* * *

Our third meeting in Cairo was at the Zoo. Except for a changed expression in her eyes, from which all the joyfulness had gone, the beautiful radiant face that day looked the same as ever. We walked for a while along the fence that shut off the grounds from the road leading up to the gates of the University—that highway of memories, unforgettable, shared.

'You know you're inflicting too much on yourself?'

'But you can't imagine how happy this makes me!' Should I have said that? 'Loneliness is terrible, Doreya. It's the worst evil anyone can suffer.' The world-weary tone I used was probably calculated.

'I haven't been to the Zoo since our student days.'

'I'm lonely as well,' I said, persisting. 'I know what it's like.'

She now had the look of a cornered animal. I was upset. My feelings were growing more twisted, more tangled, but I couldn't control myself any longer. When our eyes met it seemed to me that she flinched.

'It's wretched that I should be walking here in the fresh air, while he's . . . in there.' Then she noticed that I was very quiet. 'What's the matter?'

'I can't get over this sense of guilt.'

'I'm afraid my company will only add to your pain.'

'No. It's just that this accursed feeling feeds and thrives on despair.'

'We can try to find some comfort in seeing each other.'

'And despair ends in recklessness. Which can only add to the trouble.'

'What do you mean?'

'I mean ... I mean ... Would you forgive me if I couldn't help myself ... and told you ... that I love you now as I loved you in the past?'

I'd done it. Madness. What could I gain by it? Like someone who in order to put out the fire that's burning his clothes dives headlong into a watery abyss.

'Mansour!' The note of reproach in her voice was like a slap across the face.

'Forgive me.' My voice sounded weak. 'I can't imagine how I spoke out. But believe me, I can never find happiness, or even try to.'

As I took the train back to Alexandria I reminded myself that a man could show more courage in letters.

*   *   *

I woke up to a terrible noise, which for all I knew might have been a projection of my own troubles. But the noise outside was of a quite different kind. I left my room in time to catch the last scene of a battle and I could see from their faces that Sarhan, Zohra and another woman had been either its heroes or its victims. But who was the woman? And what did Zohra have to do with it all?

When Zohra brought my afternoon cup of tea she told me all about what had happened; how the woman had rushed in after Sarhan on his return to the *pension*, how they'd fought, and how she'd become involved as she tried to separate them.

'But who's the woman, Zohra?'

'I don't know.'

'I heard Madame say she'd been Sarhan's fiancée.'

She considered the idea for some time. 'Maybe.'

'But why should she hit you?'

'I said I was trying to separate them.'

'That's no reason why she should turn on you.'

'Well, it just happened.'

I looked at her kindly. 'Is there anything between you and ...?'

She wouldn't answer. 'There's nothing wrong in that. I'm asking you as a friend.' She nodded in reply. 'So you're engaged and keep it a secret from me?'

'No!' she said emphatically, shaking her head.

'Ah! You haven't announced your engagement yet?' Her silence worried me. 'Then when will it be announced?'

'All in good time.' She seemed confident.

I was still worried. 'But he deserted this other woman.'

She said naively, 'Because he doesn't love her.'

'Then why did they get engaged?'

She looked at me for a moment, then took courage. 'She wasn't really his fiancée. She's a fallen woman.'

'That doesn't alter his fickleness.' My own words sounded pathetic and odd in my ears; and immediately my thoughts were shot with poison. I cursed Sarhan, whom I hated as I hated myself.

A few days later she came in at the same time in the afternoon and cried out gaily, 'Mr. Mansour, shall I tell you something?'

I looked up expecting to hear something of her relationship with Sarhan.

'I'm going to learn to read and write.' I did not understand. 'I've made arrangements with one of the neighbours—Miss Aleya Mohammed, the teacher. She's going to give me lessons.'

'Really?'

'Yes, we've arranged it all.'

'That's wonderful, Zohra. How did you think of that?'

'I won't stay ignorant forever. And then I have something else in mind.'

'What?'

'That I'll learn some craft or trade, of course.'

'Good, Zohra. Excellent.' I admired her very much. I was happy for her, and pondered these feelings in my room after she'd gone.

It was raining heavily outside and the sea seemed to rage in a strange broken language. It didn't take long for the elation I'd felt a few minutes earlier to cool, condensing back into the stagnant shape of my habitual moodiness. Thus rising at once recalls falling, strength recalls weakness, innocence recalls depravity, hope recalls despair. For the second time, I had found in Sarhan the perfect object on which to project my anger. I cursed him.

*   *   *

We chose a table under a eucalyptus tree in the little café on the Nile bank, where the afternoon sun was feebly pursuing the biting cold of a Cairo winter. Avoiding my eyes all the time, she said, 'I shouldn't have come.'

'But you have,' I answered reassuringly. 'So that's decided.'

'Nothing is decided, believe me.'

I looked at her. I had to take the plunge. 'I'm sure your coming . . .'

'No. It's just that I wouldn't stay alone with your letters.'

'There's nothing new in my letters.'

'But you've written them to someone who just doesn't exist.' I touched her hand lying on the table in proof, as it were, that she did exist. She took her hand away. 'They're four years late.'

'But they tell you things that have nothing to do with time or place.'

'Can't you see that I'm weak and miserable!'

'Well so am I. Our friends see me as a spy. I see myself as a renegade, a traitor. I have no one but you.'

'Some comfort.'

'There's nothing left for me otherwise. Except madness or death.'

She sighed as if it hurt. 'I betrayed him in my mind a long time ago.'

'No. You were a classic example of false loyalty.'

'Another way of putting it.'

'We suffer for no real cause.' I explained angrily, 'That's the tragedy.' We watched the Nile, it's lead-coloured wavelets almost still. Behind the table my hand stole to hers and held it tenderly. I pressed it a little, ignoring her feeble attempts at resistance. I whispered, 'We mustn't let morbid thoughts overcome us.'

'We're falling,' she said sadly. 'Faster than I could have imagined.'

'Never mind. We'll come out of it as pure as gold.'

But I wanted to fall all the way, wanted to hit the bottom, as if to bear witness by my very self that the end-all of mankind's greed for happiness is Hell.

At the station in Cairo I ran into an old friend, a journalist who was sympathetic to progressive causes, but was careful never to dabble in politics. We sat together in the station cafe. I was waiting for my train and he was waiting for someone arriving from the Canal Zone.

'I must say I'm glad I ran into you like this. I really wanted to see you.' Marvellous. What did he want? I hadn't seen him since I'd gone to Alexandria. 'What brings you to Cairo?' I stared at him. He knew, of course, that I'd be startled at the question. 'Excuse my being so frank,' he went on, 'but I must plead our old friendship. It's rumoured that you come here for Mrs. Fawzi.'

I wasn't as upset as he expected. Doreya and I had guessed that there'd be talk.

I said coldly, 'She needs a friend, you know.'

'I also know—'

'That I was in love with her once.' I made the interruption as if I didn't care.

'What about Fawzi?'

'He's greater than they think.'

He was obviously troubled. 'As a friend of yours, I'm not very happy at what I hear people say.'

'Tell me what you've heard.' He was silent and I added nervously, 'That I'm a spy, that I ran away at the right moment, and that now I'm sneaking back to my old friend's house?'

'I only meant to . . .'

'Do _you_ believe it?'

'No, no. If you think that for a moment, I won't forgive you.'

On my way back to Alexandria I wondered if I deserved to live. What other solution was there, after all, to so many contradictions? Why shouldn't death provide the answer—a final word? I wanted to sit for a while in the Trianon, but when I saw Hosny Allam and Sarhan el-Beheiry inside talking, I decided against it. Coloured clouds driven by fresh gusts of wind raced over my head as I turned away. Along the Corniche, when the waves were rising high and cold spray was flying over the road, I walked defiantly, wishing I had something valuable in my hands, so I could smash it to bits. I said to myself that only a disaster, huge in scale, something in the order of a colossal earthquake, could bring back harmony.

*   *   *

Zohra brought in my tea. 'My people came to fetch me back,' she said, 'but I refused to go.' She spoke proudly, sure of my interest in her. And I was interested, in spite of my low spirits at the time.

'Well done!'

'Even good old Amer Bey advised me to go back home.'

'He's afraid you'll be in trouble, that's all.'

'But you're not smiling the way you always do.' She said that after she had looked at me for a while and I tried to grin at her in reply. 'I understand,' she said.

'You understand?'

'Yes. Your going away every week and your brooding.' At that I couldn't help smiling. 'I hope I'll be able to offer you congratulations and best wishes very soon!'

'May God give ear to what you say, Zohra.' We exchanged glances and she made a movement with her hands as if to lift me into happiness. 'But someone keeps spoiling things for me.'

'Who's that?'

'Someone who betrayed his faith.'

She threw up her hands in horror.

'And betrayed his friend and master.'

'Oh!'

'But he's in love. Do you suppose that could help him earn a pardon for his crime?'

She was still horrified. 'It's wicked to have no faith. A treacherous man's love is as rotten and unhealthy as he is.'

* * *

I buried myself in my work, but when I could no longer bear the stress of my shattered nerves, I would make the trip to Cairo, where I found a kind of happiness. But what kind was it? When she stopped resisting and finally surrendered herself, it's true, I was overjoyed. But afterwards I was torn by anxiety, obsessed with the morbid idea that love was the road to death and that my own excesses would destroy me.

'I'd loved you for a long time,' I said to her once. 'You remember that, don't you? Then came the shock of hearing about your engagement.'

'You've always been so diffident,' she said, with a regret that seemed to apply to both past and present. 'And that's why you're sometimes misunderstood. It was because of his strength of character that I accepted Fawzi. You know. He's an admirable man.'

The place was full of lovers.

'Are we happy?'

She looked up in surprise. 'Mansour, what a question!'

'I mean, perhaps you don't like becoming the talk of the town.'

'I don't care. As for Fawzi ...' She was going to repeat to me what I'd often told her about his tolerance, his great heart and so on, but she stopped short. I hated hearing the old story. I changed the subject.

'Doreya, did you ever suspect me the way they did?' She frowned. She had often warned me not to bring up the subject, but I couldn't help myself. 'After all, it would only have been natural ...'

'For God's sake, why do you torture yourself?'

I said with a smile, 'I often wonder why you should have thought differently.'

'The fact is, it's not in you to betray anyone.' She was annoyed.

'What's a traitor like? Certainly I'm weak or I wouldn't have given in to my brother. And it's the weak who are most likely to betray.'

She took my hand in hers. 'Please, don't torment yourself. Think of us.'

She had no idea that her love itself had now become one of my torments.

*　　*　　*

Madame came into my room and I knew I was in for some news. She flitted around with her gossip like a butterfly. 'Haven't you heard, Monsieur Mansour? Mahmoud Abu el Abbas has proposed to Zohra but she's refused him. It's madness monsieur!'

'She doesn't love him,' I said simply.

'She's set her heart in the wrong direction.' She gave me a wink. I was possessed by a strange idea about Sarhan el-Beheiry. I found myself wishing that in fact he'd really desert her so that I could punish him as I'd been longing to.

'Please speak to her,' whispered the old lady. 'She'll listen to you. She's fond of you.'

She's fond of me! I could hardly keep my temper in hand. The old cow! ('She comes from a good family, but she's no saint. Her business has its demands. If I hadn't helped her, her flat and her money would have been confiscated long ago.')

*　　*　　*

A wild wind was driving rain against the windows and the roar of the waves was shaking me to the heart. I didn't hear Zohra come in. She set the cup of tea before me on the table. I was glad to see her. I thought she might be able to rouse me out of my dark melancholy. We smiled at one another and I gave her her biscuit.

'There. You've refused another offer.' I laughed, but she just looked at me cautiously. 'To tell you the truth, Zohra, I'd recommend Mahmoud rather than Sarhan.'

She frowned. 'That's because you don't know him.'

'Do you really know the other fellow as well as you should?'

'You all think it would be beneath him to marry me.'

'But we're your friends. You shouldn't say that.'

'That Mahmoud thinks a woman is like an old shoe.'

I laughed when she told me an anecdote about Mahmoud. 'You can stand up to him all right.' But she was in love with Sarhan. She'd go on until he married her or ditched her. 'Zohra, I respect your philosophy and the way you act. Let me look forward to wishing you every happiness soon.'

* * *

A rush of urgent work held me up one week, I couldn't go to Cairo, and Doreya telephoned, complaining of her loneliness. When we met the following week she said anxiously, 'Now it's my turn to chase you.'

I kissed her hand as we entered a private room at the Florida. I explained my week's absence and gave her my news. Her nerves were on edge, and she smoked all the time. I was in no better shape.

'I've tried to drown myself in work, but I always come back to the surface in spite of myself, with a strange voice telling me that I've forgotten something important. And from time to time I really have forgotten things. In my room or in the office.'

'But I'm all by myself,' she pleaded. 'I can't stand it any more.'

'We're in a cleft stick. And we don't lift a finger to help ourselves.'

'What can we do?'

I pondered a little. The alternatives were very logical. But built on what kind of premises? I felt completely distraught. 'It just stands to simple reason: we should either separate or try to get you your divorce.' I said it challengingly, as if I were looking for even more trouble than I already had.

Her grey eyes widened in fascination as well as fear, quite possibly because she was not as repelled by this idea as she was actually allured by its brutality.

82

'Divorce!'

'Yes.' I said quietly, 'Then we could start all over again.'

'That would be mad.'

'But natural. And ethical, if you like.'

She leant her forehead on her hand and fell quiet, defeated.

'You see, you won't do a thing! Tell me,' I said after a pause, 'what would Fawzi do if he were in my place?'

'You know he loves me,' she said weakly.

'But he wouldn't hold you, if he knew you loved *me*.'

'Don't you think this is all just theoretical?'

'But I know Fawzi and what I've said is a fact.'

'Think. Imagine what he'd say.'

'That you deserted him when he went to prison? Is that it? That's not so important. You're leaving Fawzi himself, not what he stands for.' I could see him lying back on the studio sofa, watching me with his almond-shaped black eyes, smoking his pipe, discussing all kinds of problems, but never once doubting the security of his own marriage.

'What are you thinking?'

'Life gives nothing except to those who are strong enough to take.' I took her hand in mine. 'How about a drink? We've had enough thinking.'

*　　*　　*

I was almost stunned with anger. I'd heard of Hosny Allam's attack on Zohra and was seething with rage. Sitting in the drawing-room with Amer Wagdi and Madame, I couldn't hear any of their talk except as a sort of incessant buzzing. I'd also heard about a fight between Hosny and Sarhan and I sat there wishing they'd fought to the death, the two of them. I longed to teach Hosny a lesson, though I knew I stood no chance against him, which made me hate him to the point of madness.

As Madame left the room, I awoke at once from my dreams of fighting and death. Amer Wagdi was watching me, and I suddenly had the odd notion that this old man could have been a good friend of my father or my grandfather.

'What are you dreaming of?'

All I could say was, 'I think I have no future.'

He smiled gently. He knew all about it; he'd been through it all. 'Youth doesn't favour contentment,' he said. 'That's all. Really.'

'I've been so engulfed in the past that I've come to feel and believe that there is no future.'

His smile vanished and he spoke in earnest. 'Perhaps there was some shock, some lapse, or some bad luck in your case. But you're someone who undoubtedly deserves to live.'

It was repugnant to me to discuss my troubles with him, even the real ones. I changed the tack. 'And what about your own dreams, sir?'

He chuckled. 'Literal or figurative? If you mean literal, I must tell you that old men sleep so lightly that they can hardly dream. Figuratively, my dream is a gentle death.'

'Is there more than one kind?'

'The happiest death for a man is after a pleasant evening to go to sleep and simply never wake up.'

I was charmed by the old man's conversation. 'Do you believe there'll be life for you after death?'

'Yes.' He laughed. 'If you publish the material of your programme in a book.'

*   *   *

I liked the weather in Alexandria. It suited me. Not just the days of clear blue and golden sun; I also liked the occasional spells of storm, when the clouds thickened, making dark mountains in the sky, the face of morning glooming into dusk. The roads of the sky would be suddenly hushed into ominous silence. A gust of wind would circulate, like a warning cry or an orator clearing his throat; a branch would start dancing, a skirt would lift—and then it would pounce wildly, thundering as far as the horizon. The sea would rage high, foam breaking on the very curbs of the streets. Thunder would bellow its ecstasies out of an unknown world; lightning would coruscate, dazzling eyesight, electrifying the heart. The rain pouring down would hug earth and sky in a wet embrace, elements mixing their warring natures to grapple and heave as if a new world were about to be born.

Only after that would sweet peace fall on the city. The darkness would lift and Alexandria would show a face made serene by her ablutions—sparkling roads, spots of fresh dark green, a clean breeze, warm sunshine—in a tranquil awakening.

I watched the storm from behind the glass of my window panes until it finally cleared. This drama of the elements touched a sympathetic cord in my inmost heart. I had a premonition that forecast, in terms still incomprehensible to me, my personal destiny.

When the clock had moved round to strike the hour I stopped my ears against any further sense of time.

But strange sounds invaded the quiet of the room. An argument? A fight? (There's enough going on in this *pension* to keep a whole continent amused.) Something told me that as usual it concerned Zohra. A door opened noisily and the voices were now clear: Zohra and Sarhan. I leaped to my door. Face to face, with Madame in the middle, they were standing in the hall.

'That's none of your business,' Sarhan was shouting. 'I'll marry as I like. I'll marry Aleya.'

Zohra was fuming with anger, furious at the way she'd been used, at the collapse of her hopes. So the bastard had had what he'd been after and wanted to run away. I went up to him, took him by the hand and led him into my room. His pyjamas were torn and his lips were bleeding.

'She's a wild beast!'

I tried to calm him down, but he wouldn't stop.

'Can you imagine? Her Highness wants to marry me!' I tried to quiet him, but he still went on. 'The crazy bitch!'

I'd had enough of his shouting. 'Why does she want to marry you?'

'Ask her! Ask her!'

'I'm asking you.'

He looked at me, listening for the first time.

'Why? There must be some reason behind such a request.' Then he asked guardedly, 'What are you getting at?'

I shouted, 'I'm getting at the fact that you're a bastard.'

'What did you say?'

I spat in his face. 'There,' I shouted. 'I spit on you and the like of you. Traitors!'

We crashed together, pounding each other until Madame ran in to separate us. 'Please, please,' she pleaded, 'I'm fed up with all this. Settle your quarrels outside, not in my house. Please.' She took him out of the room.

*　　*　　*

My heart heavy and my mind distracted, I went to my office at the studios. A woman was sitting near my desk. It was Doreya. I couldn't speak for a moment, then my head cleared. 'Doreya! What a surprise!'

85

I smiled. I had to smile. I was supposed to be very glad to see her. I took her hand and pressed it. And indeed a sudden joy came over me, scattering the worry and fear that had been gnawing at my vitals.

She looked up at me, her face very pale.

'I might have waited for a day or two until we met, but I couldn't stand it any more. I rang you and you weren't there.'

I fetched a chair and sat down facing her, with an incomprehensible anxiety beginning to creep over me.

'Let's hope it's good news, Doreya.'

'I got a message from Fawzi,' she said, looking down. 'Through an old friend, a journalist.' My heart sank. *That* journalist. No good news here, certainly. 'He's freed me to do what I like with my future.'

My heart was pounding and though everything was clear I insisted on a detailed explanation. Strangely enough, I was excited, but curiously enough, I was far from happy. I kept asking, 'What does he mean?'

'He knows about us. Obviously.'

'But how?'

We looked at each other. I felt myself not just involved, but enmeshed in something, enchained to a point where the fact that her news had not brought me happiness or relief in the least could only make me wonder. *What's the matter?* I asked myself. Then, 'Do you think he's angry?'

She sounded a little impatient when she spoke: 'Well, he's acted as you expected him to.' I bowed my head. 'So now I want to know what you think.'

Yes, of course. Now all she wanted was my green light, and everything to go her way. I was to build her the nest I'd always longed and pleaded for. My dreams were about to come true.

But it had dawned on me that I wasn't pleased with the prospect. Not at all pleased, in fact, but worried by it, feeling neither shame nor regret for our relationship or her situation, but something that had to do with myself alone. Could I ever be happy? And supposing that I couldn't bring myself to fight for my own personal happiness? In that case what position should I take?

'Whenever you start thinking and stop responding,' she said in a rather exasperated tone, 'you make me feel so unwanted—so hopelessly alone.'

I needed more time to consider the situation. Meanwhile my anxiety had reached the point where I simply couldn't respond to

86

her feelings or bother to disguise my indifference. All at once, almost as if the spell had been broken by a sudden physical blow, I was free of her power, and over my anxious and frightened soul there now swept a black, subversive wave of cruel aversion. I must have gone mad.

'Why don't you speak?' she asked sharply.

I replied in a terribly calm voice. 'Doreya. This kind offer of his. Don't accept it.' She stared full in my face, dazed, unbelieving. Sadistically, I ignored her look of angry misery. 'Don't hesitate.'

'Is it you saying this?'

'Yes.'

'It's ridiculous. I can't understand.'

I said desperately, 'We'll try to understand later.'

'You can't leave me like this, without any explanation!'

'I have no explanation.'

Her deep grey eyes shot me a furious look. 'I'm beginning to think you're mentally deranged.'

'I deserve that.'

'Were you playing with me? All the time?'

'Doreya!'

'Tell me the truth. Was it all a lie?'

'No!'

'Then has your love for me died so suddenly?'

'No! No!'

'You can't be serious!'

'I have nothing to say. To tell the truth, I hate myself. Never get too close to a man who hates himself.'

Her staring eyes reflected her inner collapse. Contemptuously, she looked away. She was silent for a while, as if she didn't know what to do with herself. 'I've been a fool. I'll have to pay for it now.' She muttered, as if she were talking to herself, 'I could never really rely on you. How could I have forgotten that? You've just used me, with your insane impulsiveness. That's it. You're mad.'

Like a guilty but penitent child, I bore her anger meekly, and to end the scene I simply said nothing, ignoring her raging looks, her fingers tapping on the edge of my desk, her sighs as she tried to catch her breath. I would not meet her eyes. I was dead to everything. Her voice came at me, urgently.

'Have you nothing to say?'

I was immovable.

She got up, pushing back her chair, and I stood as well. She went out and I followed her outside. As we crossed the street she hurried on ahead of me. It was all too obvious that she didn't want my company.

I stopped and followed her with my eyes, as if I were watching a dream, a dream that grew larger and larger until at last it pushed reality out of sight beyond the horizon. I stood there looking after her, watching her loved and familiar figure as she walked away; and even then, even at such an absurd moment, it was clear to me that this broken creature I watched disappearing into oblivion was my first and probably my last and only love. With that disappearance I felt the beginning of my own downhill slide. And in spite of my suffering, a curious ease came over me.

*   *   *

The sea stretched out a smooth blue surface (where was that mad tempest of yesterday?), the sun as it went down touched the edges of the light clouds with fire (where were yesterday's mountains of gloom?), and the evening air played with the tips of the palm trees lining the Silsila (where were those wild, earth-shaking winds?).

I looked at Zohra's pale face, the dried tears on her cheeks, her broken look. It seemed to me that I was looking in a mirror; or rather, that this was life facing me in all its ruthless primitiveness, with its intimations of pure possibility, its thorny indomitability, and its vain beguiling hopes—those qualities manifest in the power of its eternal spirit, which maintains its attraction for both the ambitious and the desperate and offers to each his proper food. Here was Zohra, robbed of both honour and pride. Yes, I was looking into a mirror.

'I don't want to hear anything,' she warned. 'No reproaches, no remarks.'

'Just as you like.' I had not yet recovered from my experience with Doreya; I had not had time to analyse and understand it and I was still charged with it to the point of losing my mind. I knew the storm was near at hand, that I hadn't reached the catastrophe of the drama yet. I couldn't remain silent.

'It may all be for the best,' I said sympathetically. But she didn't answer. 'What are your plans for the future?'

'I am alive, as you see.'

'What about your dreams?'

'I'll go on.' She sounded determined, but where was her spirit?

'You'll get over it. You'll marry and have children.'

'I'd just better stay away from men, that's all,' she said sourly. And I laughed, for the first time in ages. She knew nothing of the tempest in my own soul or the madness stalking me.

Suddenly a notion flashed through my brain. Or was it really so new and so sudden? For it must have had deep roots in my mind, of which I'd been unconscious. Something really tempting—strange, mad, and original. For all I knew, it might be the end of my quest, the cure to my chronic troubles. I looked at her tenderly. And I said, 'Zohra, I can't bear to see you so unhappy.'

She smiled her thanks with reluctance. I was carried away on a wave of emotion. 'Zohra! Look up! Hold on to your strength, the way you used to. Tell me, when shall I see you smiling happily again?' She looked down and smiled again. Another surge of emotion carried me higher still. Here she was, lonely, dishonoured, deserted. 'Zohra, you probably don't know how dear you are to me.' I said, 'Zohra, marry me.'

She turned suddenly, startled, unbelieving, and opened her lips to speak but couldn't make a sound. I went on, still under the influence of my insanity. 'Please take me, Zohra! I mean it.'

'No!'

'Let's get married as soon as we can!'

Her fingers moved nervously and she said, 'You're in love with another woman.'

'There was no love. You just imagined it. Please answer me.'

She took a deep breath, watching my face suspiciously. 'It's kind and decent on your part. Your pity's got the better of you. Thank you. But I can't accept. And you don't mean it. Please don't mention it again.'

'You refuse me?'

'Thank you very much. But just forget it.'

'Believe me. I mean it. Give me a promise, a hope and I'll wait.'

'No.' She spoke firmly, obviously not believing a word of what I'd said. 'Thank you for all your kindness. I really appreciate it, but I can't accept it. Go back to your girl. If there's anything wrong, it must be her fault and you'll soon forgive her.'

'Zohra, please believe me.'

'No! Stop it. Please!' She sounded adamantly firm, but her eyes showed how tired she was. And as if she couldn't bear the situation any longer, she thanked me with a nod of her head and left the room.

Rebounding back into emptiness, I looked around like a drowning man. When would the earthquake come? When would the storm begin to blow? What had I said? And how could I possibly have said it? Why? Was there some mysterious double who put words in my mouth at his will? How could I put a stop to it all?

How can I put a stop to it? I repeated the question obsessively as I left the room.

In the hall Sarhan was on the telephone. His suitcase stood near the door, announcing his final departure. I looked with loathing at the back of his head, bent to the receiver, hating him with an intensity that seemed inevitable. He occupied a greater place in my life than I had imagined. What would I do with my life if he disappeared altogether. How would I find him again? I would be unable to keep myself from following him, tracking him down: *Sarhan is the poisoned cup that would cure me.*

'Good!' he shouted down the receiver. 'Eight o'clock! I'll wait for you at the Swan!'

It was a date. He was giving me a direction and a goal. His self-assured voice drew me to destruction, commanding me to follow him. He would serve me, deliver me.

*　　*　　*

I went to the Atheneus and thought of writing a letter to Doreya, but my agitation got the better of everything, my will, my mind.

At the Swan, I took a seat in the furthest corner of the inner hall, like an emigrant packed, ready, awaiting his departure, who has completely washed his hands of the city and all its cares. My brain began to clear. I drank two cognacs, my eyes riveted on the entrance.

At a quarter to eight my quarry arrived, in the company of Tolba Marzuq. Had he been the man on the phone? When had this chance friendship started? They sat down on the other side of the hall. I watched them drink their cognac. I remembered that I had agreed at breakfast to Tolba Marzuq's suggestion that we spend New Year's Eve at the Monseigneur. I had promised to celebrate the New Year! I watched them from my corner, drinking, talking, laughing.

I take care not to let him see me, but he gets a glimpse of me in the mirror. I ignore him and go out cursing. The road is completely deserted. And then I hear his shoes creaking behind me. I slow my pace until he almost catches up with me. We have gone quite a distance down the deserted road. He comes up to me and slackens his stride, not wishing to expose his defenceless back to me.

'You've been following me! I spotted you from the start.'

I say curtly, 'Yes.'

'Why?' he asks warily.

'To kill you,' I say, taking the scissors out of my coat.

His eyes stare at the scissors. 'You must be crazy.'

We put ourselves on guard, braced, ready to attack or defend.

'You're not her keeper, are you?'

'It's not just for Zohra. Not just for Zohra.'

'What is it then?'

'For life. My life. I have no life if I don't kill you.'

'But you'll be killed too. Can't you see that?'

I am completely detached. The emigrant feeling comes over me again and I delight in it.

'How did you know where I was?' he asks without warning.

'I heard you talking on the phone at the Pension.'

'And made up your mind to kill me?'

'Yes.'

'You never thought of that before?' I flinch and make no reply, but do not back down. 'You don't really want to kill me?'

'I do. And I will.'

'Supposing you hadn't seen me or heard me when I was on the phone?'

'I did see and I did hear. And I'm going to kill you.'

'But why?'

I flinch again. But my desire to kill him grows stronger and stronger. 'That's why!' I cry, stabbing at him. 'Take this. And this!'

As he talked to Tolba Marzuq I heard Sarhan laugh. He left the table a number of times, but always eventually returned to his seat. I cursed Tolba Marzuq, his coming had spoilt everything. But after an hour or so he left. Sarhan stayed alone at the table, and I grew impatient for the moment of my deliverance.

He went on drinking, but kept looking anxiously towards the entrance. Was he waiting for someone else? Would I miss my opportunity forever? The waiter called him to the telephone. In a few moments he came back frowning, looking, in fact, completely dejected. He did not sit down, but paid his bill and left. I watched him through the glass screen and saw him go to the bar. More drink? I waited until he went out and then I followed him slowly. When I came out of the door, he had already crossed the road.

I drew my coat close against the biting breeze. A light mist hung around the street lamps. The road was deserted and, except for the sound of the wind in the undergrowth on either side, absolutely quiet. I followed him cautiously, keeping close to the wall. But he was so completely oblivious of everything around, so absorbed in a world of his own, that he had even forgotten to put on the coat he was carrying over his arm. What was it? He'd been laughing and talking all the time. Why the sudden change? As for me, I was obsessed by one thought alone, my sole salvation.

He turned up the lonely country lane that led to the Palma, dark and empty, completely without life at that hour. *Where is he going?* I thought. *What Fate delivers him to me in this way?* For fear of losing him I hurried, keeping close to the railings of the parks, for it was pitch-dark. *I must make ready to strike,* I said to myself. But he suddenly stopped. *Something will happen, someone will come.* I was trembling all over. *I have to wait.* He made a strange sound. A word? A signal? He was vomiting. He moved slowly forward for a short distance, then fell. Stone drunk! He had drunk too much! I listened carefully, but nothing happened. Creeping closer, I almost stumbled over him in the dark. I bent over him, trying to call out his name, but the words stuck in my throat. I touched his body and his face but he did not move. He was completely unconscious. *He'll die without fear or pain,* I thought, *the death old Amer Wagdi wishes for.* I shook him gently, but he would not move. I shook him harder, violently, but there was no way of waking him up. I stood up angrily and pushed my hand into my coat pocket for the scissors.

Nothing. I looked in every pocket. Had I forgotten to take the scissors? I had been extremely upset, desperate, when Madame came in to consult me about celebrating New Year's Eve. Yes, I'd left the room without taking what I'd come for.

I was furious at myself and at this drunk enjoying an oblivion he didn't deserve. I kicked him in the ribs once, twice, brutally, then I was kicking him like a lunatic, everywhere, until my anger and excitement were spent and I fell back panting against the iron railing, saying to myself, *I've finished him. I've finished him!* I was nauseated, barely able to breathe, obsessed by the thoughts of my own madness.

I was insane. A madman behaving madly in the dark. And there was Doreya, gazing into my eyes, disappearing among the crowd in the street.

I walked back to the *pension*, imagining Zohra sleeping, a heavy oppressive sleep. Then I took a sleeping pill and threw myself on the bed.

He was shoving me with a hand on my shoulder. My brother. I shouted back at him. 'You've broken me for good!'

4. SARHAN EL-BEHEIRY

The High-Life Grocery. What a brilliant spectacle for the gourmet and the epicure—bright lights playing over jars of *hors d'oeuvres*, pots of pickles, and tins of sweets, the cold meat and smoked fish, the bottles and flasks of all shapes sparkling with wines from every corner of the earth. Willy nilly, my feet want to stop in front of every Greek grocery in the city.

This time, as the ripe autumn breeze brings a heady aroma wafting into my nostrils I stand there watching a *fellaha* at the counter and thinking: Blessed be the land that fed those cheeks and those breasts of yours![58] I'd seen her as I was scrutinizing the prices on the wine bottles in the window: my eyes passed over the barrel of olives, slipped through a space between a Haig and a Dewar's, hopped across the ham slicer, and lit on the profile of her nut-brown face, which was tilted up towards the grocer with his big Balkan mustachios. She carried a straw bag full of groceries and the tip of a bottle of Johnny Walker was just peeping out at one corner.

I stood in her way as she left the shop. Our eyes met, mine smiling with admiration but hers severely questioning, then I followed close behind her, paying tribute to her country beauty. At the Corniche we were met by squalls of autumn wind, tinged with the faltering rays of the sun. She walked on in quick straight steps and when she turned in at the entrance to the Miramar building she looked back quickly: honey-brown eyes, exquisite but rigidly noncommittal.

I remembered the cotton-picking season at home.

I'd almost forgotten her when I saw her again at the end of the week. She was buying the papers at Mahmoud's stall.

'What a lovely morning!'

It was Mahmoud who responded to my greeting, but she

glanced at me and I looked her straight in the eyes, staring like a hawk, mesmerically. She hurried away, but in my senses the way she moved had already laid a charge.

'You lucky devil!' I said to Mahmoud, who laughed innocently. 'Where does she come from?'

'She works in the Pension Miramar,' he said indifferently.

I paid back some money I'd borrowed from him to send home and walked round the fountain waiting for Engineer Ali Bakir.

What a sweet *fellaha*, absolutely delicious: there she goes, pulling my vitals after her. The whole world delighted me—the excitement of my own desires, the softness of the sunlight, with the multitude of faces I saw waiting around me. And I remembered again the cotton-picking season at home.

* * *

Ali Bakir turned up about ten. I took him to my flat in Sharia Lido in Mazarita. Safeya was ready and we went to the Metro cinema. At one in the afternoon we came out. They went straight on to the flat, while I went to the High-Life to get a bottle of Cyprus wine.

At the counter shopping, as my fantastic dream-like good luck would have it, stood the *fellaha*, again. Something made her sense that I was behind her: she turned her head, met my smiling face, and looked away. In a mirror in the middle of the wine bottles, though, I caught a glimpse of a smile forming on her rose-pink lips. Like a daydreamer I could see myself living in the *pension*, wallowing in the warmth of her love. She had crept into my soul, stirring my heart the way it had been stirred only once before, in college. That bright and candid smile, like the sun! A peasant girl, away from home, alien in that *pension*, like a faithful dog astray, looking for its master.

'If it weren't broad daylight I'd drive you home,' I said as we went out of the shop side by side.

'*You* don't underrate yourself!' She wasn't really being angry. As I made my way back to our place, I had sweet visions of the country, of virgin love.

Ali Bakir was sitting cross-legged on a cushion. Safeya was cooking in the kitchen. I threw myself down next to Ali and set the bottle before him. 'It's an inferno. That's the latest scientific definition of the current price situation.'

He laid his hand on my arm. 'I suppose you've managed to get your family through the usual school-opening crisis?'[59]

95

'Yes, but not without suffering for it.' I had told him that I'd given up the rent from my share of the inheritance to my mother and brothers, but four *feddans* couldn't go far.

'You're still young,' he said encouragingly. 'You have a brilliant future before you.'

But I was bored with that kind of talk. 'Let's stay with the present, if you don't mind. What's life worth without your own villa, your own car, and your own woman'?'

He laughed in agreement, but Safeya heard me as she was bringing in the tray and shot me a searing look.

'He's got everything he needs,' she said to the engineer. 'But he's a hard-hearted son of a bitch.'

I retreated. 'The fact is I have nothing but the woman.'

'We've been living together for over a year,' she said in her nagging fashion. 'I thought I'd teach him to be careful with money, but he's taught me how to throw it away.'

We ate and drank. Then we slept. In the evening the three of us went out, Safeya to the Genevoise, Ali Bakir and I to the Café de la Paix.

'Does she still hope she can marry you?' he asked as we sipped our coffee.

'She's out of her mind. What can you expect from a nut?'

'I'm worried ...'

'She's got her head in the clouds. Besides, I'm sick of her.'

Through the glass window we looked out at a sunny evening. I felt Ali Bakir's eyes turned on me, but I ignored them. I knew what was coming

'Now let's get serious,' he suddenly said.

I looked at him. We were facing each other. It was too late. There was no way out.

'Right. Let's get serious.'

'Fine. The plan's been thoroughly gone over from beginning to end.' He was unnervingly calm.

My heart contracted. I looked at him, surrendering, drawn on even though full of misgivings.

'Now I'm the superintendent. You're responsible for the accounts and books. The lorry-driver is safe and so is the guard. Nothing is left but for the four of us to get together and swear on the Koran.'

I laughed out loud. He looked at me, surprised, then realized how ridiculous what he'd just said was.

'All right.' He laughed in return. 'Even so, we'll take an oath.

The goods are up for grabs. You can imagine what a lorry load of yarn can make on the black market. It's a safe operation and we can repeat it four times a month.'

What he said made me thoughtful and I let my mind drift.

'Believe me,' he went on, 'there's no other way. Doing it legally is running after nothing. You get a promotion or a bonus now and then. So what! You can't afford anything. How much does an egg cost? How much do you have to pay for a suit? Even for food! And you're talking about a car, a villa and a woman. All right. Buy all that. Look, you were elected to the ASU Base Unit and to the Board of Directors. What did it all come to? You volunteered to arbitrate for the workers and solve their problems. Did they give you anything? Did they open the doors of Heaven for you? Prices are going up, salaries are going down. And life is going by. Great! There's something wrong somewhere! How did it happen? Are we being used for guinea pigs? Baby, just turn my face to the wall!'[60]

'When do we start?' My own voice sounded strange in my ears.

'We won't start for another month or two. We have to plan all the details very, very carefully. Afterwards you'll live the life of good old Haroun el-Rasheed.'

I still felt very edgy, even though I'd really given in to him long before.

'Eh? What do you say?' He looked me sharply in the eye.

I burst out laughing. I laughed until the tears came; and he sat there, his cold face set, eyes fixed on me all the while. I leaned across the table. 'Okay,' I whispered, 'chum!'

He shook me by the hand and left. As I sat there alone I was torn by all kinds of ideas. I remembered an incident with Mahmoud Abu el Abbas, a few days before.

'*Ustaz*,'[61] he said, 'I'll soon be needing your help and experience.'

'What for?'

'God willing, I'll buy Panayoti's restaurant when he sells out and leaves.'

I was astounded. Had he made enough money out of the newsstand to buy a little restaurant? 'What can I do for you? All I know about food is that we eat it.'

'No. Just teach me how to keep the books.'

I promised finally to help him.

The thought crossed my mind that I might sell the few *feddans* I had and come in as his partner. 'You'll probably need a partner,' I said.

97

But he obviously disliked the idea. 'No, I prefer to work on my own. I'd rather keep it a small business and not attract the attention of the government.'

* * *

I'd been to the headquarters of the Socialist Union where I'd listened to a talk on the black market, followed by a discussion. As I was leaving the hall at the end of the meeting, I heard someone call my name. I stopped, looked around, and saw Rafat Amin making his way towards me in the crowd. I hadn't seen him since we'd been together at college. We shook hands cordially and pushed through the throng together out to the road. He said he'd attended the meeting because he too was a member of the Base Unit of the Socialist Union, at the Amalgamated Metallurgies. It was a pleasant evening, so we walked in the direction of the Corniche. When we finally found ourselves alone in the street, we burst out laughing at the same time, for no apparent reason, but because of memories we shared, memories we couldn't forget or ignore — the number of meetings we'd been to where we'd clapped and cheered together. We'd both been members of Wafdist Student Committees. *Do you remember? Sure! Who can forget those days?* Then we were in opposition to the State. Now we *are* the State!

'I can't imagine that you of all people should have turned your back on your precious Wafdism!' he said, laughing all over again.

'And what about you? You couldn't have been a loyal Wafdist. Tit for tat and you started it.'

'But you! *Are* you a real socialist?' he asked, nudging me with his elbow.

'Of course.'

'Why, if you don't mind telling me?'

'Even the blind can see the achievements of the Revolution.'

'But you're not blind, are you?'

'I mean it,' I said seriously.

'So you're a revolutionary socialist?'

'Certainly.'

'Congratulations. Now tell me where we can spend the evening.'

I took him to the Genevoise. At midnight I wanted to wait for Safeya, but she said she was going out with a Libyan customer.

* * *

I was just coming out of the Strand Cinema when I saw the pretty *fellaha* coming down Safeya Zaghloul Street in the company of an old Greek woman. Dark, soft, with bewitching eyes and a ripe figure. The pavement was crowded. A cool salt-laden breeze was blowing; and a halo of clean carded cotton covered the dome of the sky, giving the air a purity and softness that perched on the heart like happiness itself. The two women threaded their way through the crowd. I stepped back to make way for them, greeting the girl with a slight nod and a flicker of my eyelids. Cautiously, she smiled. Good, I said to myself. A cautious smile, there's something in that. I was so pleased; it was like the sweet taste of green beans in my mouth, virgin-fresh, just picked out of the green fields.

* * *

I looked at her face at dusk as I drank my coffee. Her eyes were red and swollen after a long sleep, her thick lips slack. Looking her worst, as usual in the early evening, she didn't know what I had in store for her.

'Safeya?' I put as much sorrow in my tone as I could. She looked up. 'I'm in a fix. There's a stupid situation we have to face together.' She shot me a wary glance and gestured to me to explain. 'We'll have to change our way of life. I mean living together in the same flat.' She frowned and looked up, ready for a fight. 'It's a catastrophe. Especially in light of the housing shortage. But one of my colleagues gave me a hint yesterday. You must remember, surely, that I told you about the Administrative Survey? They pry into everything, they've been asking questions. I'm sure you care about my career as much as I do.'

'But we've been living together for a year and a half,' she protested.

'They've been the happiest days of my life. We might have gone on forever without anybody knowing. But ...' I looked into my empty cup as if I were reading my fortune '... but I'm out of luck. It seems I'll just have to go back to living on my own in a messy bachelor flat. I may even have to live in some dirty little hotel or noisy *pension*.'

'There *is* a way!' she hissed. 'You *know* there is. Only you're an ungrateful bastard!'

'I've been honest. I told you from the beginning: I'm not the marrying kind. I'll always love you, but God didn't design me for marriage.'

'Because he made you without a heart.'

'In that case there's no use in going over all this again.'

She looked me deep in the eyes. 'You want to leave me?'

'Safeya, stop it. If that were the case, I'd have said it right out a long time ago.'

She was terribly upset; and her grimaces added to the ugliness of her face at the moment. I wished she'd hate me and let me go my own way.

We're through, I thought. I said to myself that on Judgement Day we'd balance each other in the scales. *We've shared everything except her presents to me on special occasions, which I couldn't return because of my commitments at home. Other men exploit their mistresses shamelessly. True, I'm not used to spending money on women. In any case I expect a final battle. I've been through all this before. I really fell in love once at college, but I'd arrived on the scene too late. It would have been a wonderful match—a beautiful girl with a great future, the daughter of a rich doctor, rolling in money from his patients. But what's the use of that now? It's too late. Anyway, I've fallen again. Yes, I think I love the fellaha, though it's just a physical attraction, I suppose, like the one that led me to Safeya at the Genevoise.*

*　　*　　*

'I'd like a room for a long stay.'

Her inquisitive blue eyes gleam with satisfaction. She leans back on the sofa under a statue of the Madonna, an air about her of faded gentility, her peroxide hair suggesting a desperate clinging to the past. She haggles shamelessly over the price of a room and insists that I should pay a higher price when summer comes.

'But have you just arrived in Alexandria?'

It isn't simply a passing question, but one in a series of enquiries. I respond by giving her an account of my work, my age, my home town and my marital status.

As we are talking the *fellaha* comes in. She blushes and looks down, taking in the situation at a glance. Madame doesn't notice the girl's confusion or her heightened colour. By the time she shows me the room, the last vacant one overlooking the street, we're like two old friends.

I like the room and sit comfortably in the big armchair. I can hear her call the girl, so I get to know her name without asking. She comes in shortly to make up the bed with fresh sheets and blankets. I watch her happily, examining her closely, at my ease, the hair, the fine features of the face, and the tall figure. My God! What a beauty! Bewitching! And she has character too! She tries to steal a look at me, but I am on the alert. I smile at her confusion.

'I am so happy, Zohra!' She goes on with her work as if she hasn't heard. 'God bless you! You've reminded me of my home in the country.' She smiles. 'Let me introduce myself. Sarhan el-Beheiry at your service.'

'A Beheiry?' she asks.

'From Farquasa in Beheira.'

'I'm from Zayadiya,' she says, biting off a smile.

'Fancy that!' I exclaim happily, as if the fact that we come from the same province is a good omen for love.

She has finished her work and is going out, but I beg her:

'Please stay a little. I have so much to tell you.'

She shakes her head with innocent coquetry and leaves. I am pleased with her refusing me; I consider it something special. She couldn't have treated an ordinary lodger so. All I have to do now is put out my hand and pluck. Her body looks innocent, though; and I don't know if she'd be willing or not.

I love her and can't do without her. I wish we were together somewhere, away from this *pension*, which must be full of tiresome, inquisitive fools.

At breakfast I am introduced to two strange old men. One of them, Amer Wagdi, is so old he's an actual mummy, but he's a merry old fellow. They say he's an ex-journalist. The other is Tolba Marzuq, whose name sounds vaguely familiar. He's under sequestration. I don't know what brings him to the *pension*, but I'm keenly interested in him from the start; anything out of the ordinary is interesting, a criminal, a madman, someone under a sentence or under sequestration. He keeps his eyes on his cup, avoiding my looks. Out of caution, I wonder, or pride? I stare at him with mixed feelings, a sense of triumph over his class mixed with pity for his individual plight. But I'm strangely alarmed at the thought of the state confiscating property. After all, it could happen to anyone.

Amer Wagdi compliments me on being an economist. 'The state now depends mainly on economists and engineers,' he says courteously. But the thought of Ali Bakir grips and depresses me. 'In my time it was the eloquent speech-makers who carried the day.' I laugh sarcastically, but the old man is hurt. Apparently he has merely stated it as a fact and not as a piece of criticism, but he goes on to defend his generation. 'My son,' he protests, 'it was our task to wake the people after a long sleep. You need words, words for that. Not economics or engineering.'

'Your generation has honourably fulfilled its duty,' I say by way of apology, 'or we wouldn't be able to do ours.'

Tolba Marzuq, the other old man, says nothing throughout the entire conversation.

My heart has recovered an innocence as youthful as this beautiful morning, the clear blue sea, and the blessed warmth of the sun. A kind of vigour seems to sing in my blood: my love for life expands with every breath I take. I work well at the plant, then have lunch with Safeya in my old flat. She gives me a penetrating look and I put on the mask of depression. I complain of my loneliness at the *pension*. 'I don't think I can stand it for long, darling. I've asked a house-agent to try and get me a flat.' I hear the old song about being an ungrateful bastard. In bed with her after lunch, I wonder when I'll be released from this hard labour.

Later back at the *pension* I see Zohra carrying a cup of coffee to Amer Wagdi's room. The clock strikes five, so I order a cup of tea. She comes in blooming like a flower or a song, a melody of black hair, dark skin and delectable eyes. I touch her hand as she gives the cup.

'I am a prisoner in this room,' I whisper, 'for your sake.'

She frowns to disguise her excitement and turns away.

'I love you!' I call out after her, 'Don't forget that ever.'

The next afternoon she responds to my attempts at drawing her into conversation. I want all the information about her I can get.

'What brought you here from Zayadiya?'

'I had to make a living,' she says in her homely country accent. She tells about her people, her running away from home and finding refuge with Madame, an old client of her father.

'But she's a foreigner. And the *pension* is almost a market place, you know.'

'I have worked in the fields,' she replies proudly, 'and in the markets.'

The girl is no fool. But should I take her story at its face value? Village girls who run away from home have usually left something behind.

'It all happened,' I say, dazzled by her, 'so that we might meet in this *pension*.'

She looks at me curiously and not unsuspiciously, but cannot disguise her liking for me.

'I love you! I can't stop telling you that over and over again, Zohra.'

'That's enough,' she murmurs.

'No! I won't stop it until I hear the same words from your lips, and have you safe in my arms.'

'Is that what you're up to?'

'Yes. Otherwise I can find no pleasure in life.'

She is not angry or upset, but leaves me with an untroubled face. I congratulate myself. And I find myself feeling my old longing for marriage overflowing like water over a fountain's rim. I wish with all my heart I could, Zohra, but ... if ... damn all those stupid deadly obvious facts and figures!

*　　　*　　　*

Two new guests come to stay at the Miramar, Hosny Allam and Mansour Bahy. I look forward to making their acquaintance. I have a sort of hunting instinct that makes me want to add new friends or acquaintances to my bag indefatigably.

Hosny Allam comes from an old family of Tanta. A gentleman of property. He has a hundred *feddans,* is handsome, tall and powerfully built, just what we'd all love to be. I may hate his class in the abstract, but I'm fascinated by any of them, if I'm lucky enough to keep him company. It's easy to imagine the kind of life Hosny leads in spite of everything. If he's as open-handed as he ought to be, we'll have lots of good nights out together.

Mansour Bahy is quite different, a broadcaster at the Alexandria Broadcasting Service and the brother of a really big man in the police. Which is good—could be useful in fact—but he's very introverted; he has very delicate features and is as innocent as a child, but cold as a statue. Where's the key to his character? How could I find out what his real feelings are? I get so many applications for help from people from home looking for jobs here that I could do with an extra friend or two. Besides, a high police official can come in useful in lots of situations.

*　　　*　　　*

I grab her. I wait until she sets the cup of tea on the table, then grab her by the arm. She loses her balance and falls into my lap as

I sit down in the big arm chair. I take her in my arms and kiss the curve of her cheek—all I can see of her face—a quick, hungry, hurried kiss. She disentangles herself, her strong hands pushing me off, then jumps up and moves swiftly away. I look at her expectantly and smile.

Her expression softens like the sea on a mellow autumn morning. I beckon her nearer, but she won't come nearer. And yet she doesn't run away. Mad with desire I leap up and take her again in my arms. She hardly resists. Our lips meet in a long hungry kiss, the smell of her hair filling my nostrils. 'Come to me tonight,' I whisper.

She looks hard at me. 'What do you want?'

'I want *you*, Zohra.' Her eyes are serious as she stands there in front of me. 'Will you come?'

'What do you want from me?' she asks sharply. The way she says it sobers me a little.

'We'll talk,' I reply lamely, 'and make love.'

'But we're doing that now.'

'Yes, but there's too much haste, too much fear. That spoils everything.'

'I don't trust you.'

'But you don't understand me, Zohra!'

She tosses her head sceptically. But in spite of all that, she walks out of the room smiling.

I'm miserable. If only she came from some important family or had education or money. I let out a stream of curses.

*   *   *

I thought I'd spend the evening of Umm Kulthum's concert at Ali Bakir's, to listen to the music in the kind of quiet that it requires, and Rafat Amin has also invited me to his place. But after some reflection I opt for the *pension*, to consolidate my relations with the other lodgers.

There's a big tray of shish kebab and I need a quick drink or two to prepare myself for the attack. I speak at length of the glory of the Beheiry family, and of the importance of my post as Deputy Accountant, not for mere boasting's sake but to prepare them for the signs of wealth I'll be showing when Ali Bakir's plans come through. But they will talk politics; there is no avoiding the subject. Have you heard? What do you think? To tell you the truth ... and so on and so on. I can see that for them I represent the Revolution,[62] though Mansour might come in for a share. We all praise the Revolution, of course, and drink to its future.

I catch a glimpse of Zohra. She's the one who's all in favour of the Revolution. I remember how she prayed for it one day in my hearing, and how touched I was at the sincerity and fervent innocence of her prayer.

Does Mansour Bahy, I wonder, have his doubts about my sincerity? My friend, can't you see that here I am, a natural enemy of the enemies of the Revolution, and that it's been a very good thing for me?

'Well, they've closed as many doors as they've opened.'

'Think of the masses.'

'All right. But what about the greedy ones who are living in the lap of luxury?'

'People like that are the real enemies of the Revolution. You shouldn't judge by their example.'

I am sincerely fond of Madame Mariana; not just because she loves our music, but because I like her quick wit and her stories of the past, which she repeats with true unquenchable Greek nostalgia. And through those reminiscences, her old love stories and her weakness for the easy life, I can easily identify her with myself: her people are basically nomads, content to find a home wherever they can find happiness.

Amer Wagdi is a most interesting piece of antiquity. Discovered by Professor Mansour Bahy—a monument to a fascinating period of our history of which (alas!) we know very little.

When Tolba Mazuq joins in our praise of the Revolution, I can only salute this delectable hypocrisy, thinking how true it is that mankind is up to its ears, for all its conquests and inventions, in folly and stupidity.

It strikes me that it would be a good idea in general to bring a few enemies together from time to time and make them spend a long evening drinking and enjoying good music in each other's company.

'So you don't believe in Heaven and Hell?'

'Heaven is any place where you live in dignity and peace. Hell is simply the opposite.'

When Mansour laughs at one of my jokes he's like a charming child. I begin to have hopes that I may soon find out what really makes him tick, and that by the end of this musical evening we'll have become fast friends.

As for Hosny Allam—long live Hosny Allam! He has single-handedly donated two bottles of Dewar's to this evening's entertainment and is sitting square in his seat like a country squire, filling our glasses, laughing uproariously. When he suddenly disappears at midnight, the evening suffers something of a blow.

I cannot enjoy the singing the way I usually do, nor do I join in singing any of the verses of Umm Kulthum's songs. All my potential for ecstasy is focused on Zohra and whether she moves about serving us or sits in smiling wonder by the screen to watch us laugh and drink, a rich current seems to flow secretly between us. Our eyes meet stealthily, often, and though far apart, we secretly embrace and exchange lovers' kisses and torments.

*　　*　　*

I must have seen that man before. He was walking to the Trianon from the direction of Saad Zaghloul Street, while I was coming from the Square. It was Tolba Marzuq. I'd never seen him in his outdoor clothes, the thick coat, the dark red tarboosh and the scarf. I shook his hand respectfully and pressed him to take a cup of coffee. We sat behind the closed glass doors on the sea-front side of the café. The wind was playing with the crests of the palms that circled the statue of Saad Zaghloul. The sky was covered with light clouds, their fringes lambent at the touch of the sun.

We exchanged a few commonplaces. I did my best to show him deep respect and sympathy. He can't be completely broke, I thought. There must be a way of getting his confidence. He may want to make an investment, but is afraid to show that he's got any money left. I led the conversation around to the rising cost of living.

'A young man like me can't possibly depend on a government salary to get by.'

'What can he do?'

'I am thinking,' I said in a low confessional voice, 'of starting some business.'

'Where would you get the money?'

'I'd sell a few *feddans* and find a partner.' I put on an innocent smile.

'But are you allowed to go into business and keep your government job?'

'No!' I said with a smile. 'The business would have to be a secret.'

106

He wished me lots of luck, then spread out his paper as if he'd entirely forgotten I was there. *Maybe he really has nothing left. Or is it just a manoeuvre?* Anyway I lost all hope of getting anything out of him.

Pointing to a red headline about some news of Eastern Germany, he said suddenly, 'I suppose you've heard about how poor *they* are, particularly when compared with West Germany.' I agreed. He was talking domestic politics now, using the language of foreign affairs. 'Russia has nothing to offer her satellites. But the United States . . .'

'We've had really valuable aid from Russia, though.'

'That's different,' he said hastily. 'We are not a Russian satellite.' He was on his guard. I regretted what I'd said. 'Russia and the United States both wish to dominate the world,' he went on. 'Our stand of non-alignment is really the best policy and the wisest.' I'd lost him and I knew I couldn't get him back soon. I was sorry about that.

'In fact, if it hadn't been for the July Revolution the country would have been overwhelmed by bloodshed.'

He nodded his tarboosh in assent. 'God is great. His wisdom be praised, which alone has saved us!'

* * *

'Where've you been? Why, we haven't seen Your Highness for three days! So you've finally remembered me! But then why should you remember something you've thrown away? Didn't I say you were an ungrateful bastard? Don't give me any of your silly excuses. Don't tell me about your fantastically important work. Even a minister of state wouldn't neglect his mistress the way you've been neglecting me.'

I smile complacently as I pour wine in our glasses, keeping down my loathing. I can't stand her and now that she's playing the dictator, I've simply got to get rid of her—free myself from her once and for all.

* * *

Every worry in the world goes away when I see Zohra bring in my cup of tea.

We hold each other in a long embrace. I kiss her mouth, her cheeks, her forehead and her neck, then with deeper awareness I relish her lips as she presses them against mine. She draws back a little, sighing, then says, 'I think sometimes that they all know.'

'Let them!' I am reckless with the ecstasy of love.

'*You* don't care, but . . .'

'I only care for one thing, Zohra.' I look at her so that my eyes can tell her how I really feel. I plead. 'Let's live together. Away from here.'

'Where?' she asks suspiciously.

'In a home of our own.'

She waits for me to go on but when I add nothing to my proposal, her eyes cloud with disappointment. 'What do you mean?'

'You love me as I love you.'

'I love you,' she says in a low voice, 'But you don't really love me.'

'Zohra!'

'You look down on me, just the way they all do.'

'I love you. God is my witness,' I say with total sincerity. 'I love you with all my heart.'

She muses sadly for a moment. 'Do you consider me your equal as a human being?'

'Why, of course.' She shakes her head. I understand what she's getting at. 'There are problems one can't solve.'

She still shakes her head, looking upset now. 'I had to face problems at home, but I didn't give in.'

I hadn't imagined she was so proud. I feel desire driving me to the brink of an abyss, I even let my foot slip over the edge, and at the last second try to save myself, as it were, by throwing all my weight backwards. I take her hand in mine, kiss its back, its palm, and whisper in her ear, 'I love you, Zohra!'

*   *   *

When I look at Hosny Allam's strong and handsome face I always think of wonderful nights on the town. When I hear that he's come to Alexandria to start a business, though, my attitude towards him changes immediately. Tolba Marzuq is only a phantom and I'd better drop him. But Hosny is a man determined to work, to achieve something, and what I must do is find myself a part to play in his project. It's not just a question of work or success: he might save me at the last moment from Ali Bakir's God-forsaken plans. The pity of it is that Hosny is so mercurial you can hardly catch hold of him. He talks about his projected business once or twice, but he's always daydreaming, dashing around in his car, driving at a ridiculous speed—and always with some woman or other in the seat beside him.

'A man of the world,' I advise him, 'doesn't spend his time just fooling around.'

'How does he spend it?' he asks with amusement.

'Well,' I say earnestly, 'he studies a plan, considers all the angles, then goes into action.'

'Fine, but I prefer to do my studying and considering while I'm playing. We're living on the eve of Doomsday.' And he roars with laughter.

My God! I moan inwardly in despair. *I want to make good and help someone else do the same. What shall I do?*

*   *   *

It was a terrible fight. She fired her insults at me and I exploded in anger.

'Can't you forget it for once? Is it Judgement Day already?'

The insults flew back and forth between us, we bombarded each other with curses, and Mahmoud Abu el Abbas stood there dumbfounded. He had gone with me to her flat for his third lesson in arithmetic and bookkeeping. I got up determined to leave and he followed me out. At the gate of the building, I asked him to go and tell her I wasn't coming back.

I went to the Miramar but didn't realize that she had followed me until I was at the door of the flat, when I felt a hand on the back of my neck and heard Safeya shouting, 'You think you can throw me over like that? What do you take me for? A kid? A toy?'

I struggled to get away from her, but she was already inside the door.

'Go away!' I hissed, struggling for breath. 'You're disturbing the lodgers. Everyone's asleep.'

'You think you can rob me and get away with it!' she screamed. 'I've fed you and clothed you and now you want to run away from me, you pig!'

I slapped her, she slapped me back and we wound up in a scuffle. Zohra tried to break it up, but couldn't. 'Please stop that,' she said to Safeya. 'This is a respectable house.'

It didn't do any good. She threatened. 'Will you go? Or shall I call the police?'

Safeya stepped back and looked at Zohra in surprise. Then she looked from Zohra to me, drew herself up and said, 'A servant. How dare you . . .?'

Before she could finish, Zohra slapped her across the mouth. Safeya hit back, but the girl was too strong for her and hit her until she almost collapsed. Everybody was awake, doors were opened and steps came along the corridor. Hosny Allam was the first. He took Safeya by the hand and led her out.

I went to my room, blind with rage. Madame followed me there, very upset. I apologized to her, but she wanted to know who the woman was. I had to tell a lie in order to save face.

'She was my fiancée and I've broken the engagement.'

'Her behaviour shows you were right to break with her,' she said, shaking her head. 'But please settle accounts with her somewhere else. I live on the good name of my *pension*.'

When Zohra came in, her face still carried traces of the fight. I thanked her and apologized for what she had suffered. We exchanged anguished looks and I had to explain.

'I left her for you.'

'Who is she?' she asked curtly.

'A loose woman! I knew her a long time ago. But that's all over and done with. I had to tell Madame she'd been my fiancée.'

I kissed her cheek lightly, grateful, regretful.

* * *

Outside the wind roars. Inside, even though it's still only early afternoon, my room exudes evening. My mind pictures the dense clouds outside and the mounting waves of the sea. Zohra comes in and switches on the light. I haven't seen her since yesterday and I've been in torment waiting for her.

'Let's go away, Zohra,' I plead. She sets the cup on the table and looks at me with biting reproach. 'We'll live together forever. Forever.'

'And there won't be any problems then?' she asks sarcastically.

I answer with shameful frankness. 'The problems I was referring to are created by marriage.'

She mutters, 'I should be sorry I ever fell in love with you.'

'Please don't say that. Please try to understand. I love you—I can't live without you. But marriage would cause difficulties for me, with my family and at work too. It would ruin my career and that would inevitably threaten the home we make together. What can I do?'

She says even more angrily, 'I didn't realize I could bring you so much calamity.'

'It's not you! It's people's stupidity. These rigid barriers, these stinking facts! What can I do?'

'What can you do indeed?' she says, her eyes narrow with rage. 'Turn me into a woman like the one from yesterday?'

'Zohra!' I say desperately. 'If you loved me as much as I love you, you'd understand me better.'

'I do love you,' she says acidly. 'It's a mistake I can't help.'

'Love is stronger than everything. Everything.'

'Everything except your problems,' she says contemptuously.

We look at each other, feverish and desperate, furious and inflexible. If it wasn't for my fear and my strength of will, I might give in. I think quickly, in a flash. 'Zohra, there are compromises. There's the Islamic marriage in its pure original form.' Curiosity replaces anger in her eyes. I really know very little about the subject, but I go on. 'We marry as the first Muslims used to marry.'

'How was that?'

'I solemnly declare in the company of us two that I take you for my wife, according to the commandments of God and the doctrines of His Prophet.'

'With no witnesses?'

'God is our witness.'

'Everyone else around us behaves as if they didn't believe in His existence.' She shakes her head stubbornly. 'No.'

*   *   *

She's really mulish. It hasn't been as easy as I expected. There's no persuading her. If she consents to live with me, I'm ready to give up the prospect of marriage, including my plans of advancement through a suitable match. I've thought of leaving the *pension* as a first step to getting her out of my mind, but I can't. We haven't quarrelled; she still brings in my tea as usual, and lets me kiss her or take her in my arms.

One afternoon I am stunned to see her sitting in the hall bent over a primary reader, deciphering the letters. I look at her incredulously. Madame is at her place under the statue of the Virgin. Amer Wagdi is in the armchair.

'Look at our scholar, Monsieur Sarhan,' exclaims Madame smiling. 'She's made an arrangement for private lessons with a neighbour, a teacher. What do you think of that?'

I am about to laugh at Madame's teasing irony when suddenly I feel genuinely impressed. 'Bravo, Zohra! Good for you.'

The old man watches me with clouded eyes. I am all at once afraid of him, I don't know why. I go out.

I am deeply moved. Some inner voice tells me that I have been taking the girl's feelings too lightly and that God will not look kindly on me. But I can't come to terms with the idea of marrying her. Love is only an emotion and you can cope with it one way or another, but marriage is an institution, a corporation not unlike the company I work for, with its own accepted laws and regulations. What's the good of going into it, if it doesn't give me a push up the social ladder? And if the bride has no career, how can we compete in the rat race, socially or otherwise? My problem is that I've fallen in love with a girl whose credentials are insufficient for that sort of thing. But if she'd accept my love without conditions I'd give up the ideal I've always had of marriage altogether.

'You've got a lot of will power, Zohra,' I say later, to give her her due. 'But it's a pity you're tiring yourself out and wasting all your wages.'

'I won't stay illiterate all my life,' she says proudly, standing on the other side of the table.

'What good will it do you?'

'I'll learn some profession. And I won't be a servant any more.'

That stabs me to the heart. I sit there tongue-tied.

'Some of my people came to fetch me home today,' she says in a new voice.

I look at her, smiling to hide my anxiety, but she ignores my expression. 'What did you tell them?'

'We settled it. I'll go back next month.'

I cry out in extreme anxiety. 'Seriously! You're going back to the old man!'

'No. He's married now.' She drops her voice. 'There's someone else.'

I catch her by the hand. 'Let's go away together. Tomorrow,' I beg. 'Today if you like . . .'

'I said I was going home next month.'

'Zohra! Have a heart.'

'That's one solution, without problems.'

'But you love me!'

'Love and marriage are two different things,' she answers angrily. 'Isn't that what you said?'

He wished me lots of luck, then spread out his paper as if he'd entirely forgotten I was there. *Maybe he really has nothing left. Or is it just a manoeuvre?* Anyway I lost all hope of getting anything out of him.

Pointing to a red headline about some news of Eastern Germany, he said suddenly, 'I suppose you've heard about how poor *they* are, particularly when compared with West Germany.' I agreed. He was talking domestic politics now, using the language of foreign affairs. 'Russia has nothing to offer her satellites. But the United States . . .'

'We've had really valuable aid from Russia, though.'

'That's different,' he said hastily. 'We are not a Russian satellite.' He was on his guard. I regretted what I'd said. 'Russia and the United States both wish to dominate the world,' he went on. 'Our stand of non-alignment is really the best policy and the wisest.' I'd lost him and I knew I couldn't get him back soon. I was sorry about that.

'In fact, if it hadn't been for the July Revolution the country would have been overwhelmed by bloodshed.'

He nodded his tarboosh in assent. 'God is great. His wisdom be praised, which alone has saved us!'

* * *

'Where've you been? Why, we haven't seen Your Highness for three days! So you've finally remembered me! But then why should you remember something you've thrown away? Didn't I say you were an ungrateful bastard? Don't give me any of your silly excuses. Don't tell me about your fantastically important work. Even a minister of state wouldn't neglect his mistress the way you've been neglecting me.'

I smile complacently as I pour wine in our glasses, keeping down my loathing. I can't stand her and now that she's playing the dictator, I've simply got to get rid of her—free myself from her once and for all.

* * *

Every worry in the world goes away when I see Zohra bring in my cup of tea.

We hold each other in a long embrace. I kiss her mouth, her cheeks, her forehead and her neck, then with deeper awareness I relish her lips as she presses them against mine. She draws back a little, sighing, then says, 'I think sometimes that they all know.'

'Let them!' I am reckless with the ecstasy of love.

'*You* don't care, but . . .'

'I only care for one thing, Zohra.' I look at her so that my eyes can tell her how I really feel. I plead. 'Let's live together. Away from here.'

'Where?' she asks suspiciously.

'In a home of our own.'

She waits for me to go on but when I add nothing to my proposal, her eyes cloud with disappointment. 'What do you mean?'

'You love me as I love you.'

'I love you,' she says in a low voice, 'But you don't really love me.'

'Zohra!'

'You look down on me, just the way they all do.'

'I love you. God is my witness,' I say with total sincerity. 'I love you with all my heart.'

She muses sadly for a moment. 'Do you consider me your equal as a human being?'

'Why, of course.' She shakes her head. I understand what she's getting at. 'There are problems one can't solve.'

She still shakes her head, looking upset now. 'I had to face problems at home, but I didn't give in.'

I hadn't imagined she was so proud. I feel desire driving me to the brink of an abyss, I even let my foot slip over the edge, and at the last second try to save myself, as it were, by throwing all my weight backwards. I take her hand in mine, kiss its back, its palm, and whisper in her ear, 'I love you, Zohra!'

*　　*　　*

When I look at Hosny Allam's strong and handsome face I always think of wonderful nights on the town. When I hear that he's come to Alexandria to start a business, though, my attitude towards him changes immediately. Tolba Marzuq is only a phantom and I'd better drop him. But Hosny is a man determined to work, to achieve something, and what I must do is find myself a part to play in his project. It's not just a question of work or success: he might save me at the last moment from Ali Bakir's God-forsaken plans. The pity of it is that Hosny is so mercurial you can hardly catch hold of him. He talks about his projected

But her lips soon give her away; I detect the shadow of a smile. 'Zohra, you devil, you've been joking.' I am tremendously relieved.

Madame comes in, drinking tea out of a cup in her hand. She sits on the bed and tells me the story of Zohra's refusing to go back home with her relations.

'Don't you think it would have been better for her to go back home?' I suggest slyly.

Madame smiles that knowing smile of a procuress. 'Her true relations are here, Monsieur Sarhan.'

I avoid her eyes, completely ignoring the implication of her remark, but guessing that a little bird has carried gossip about us from one room to another. She probably thinks worse of us than we deserve, but I'm pleased at the idea of my imaginary conquest. Zohra's obstinacy will not give an inch, though, and I ask myself when I shall have the courage to get out of the *pension*.

* * *

It's the usual afternoon scene: Madame sitting close to the radio, almost leaning her head against the set, listening to some foreign song, and Amer Wagdi helping Zohra with her lessons. Then the bell rings. It's Zohra's teacher.

'I do hope you'll excuse me. We have visitors upstairs. If you don't mind, I'd rather give the lesson down here.'

Very courteous indeed. We make her welcome. She's quite good-looking; she is also smartly dressed, a career girl. I watch her teach Zohra and I find myself comparing the two of them, simplicity and ignorance, beauty and poverty on the one hand, with education, elegance, and a career on the other. If only Zohra could have found herself in this other girl's world, with all its potentialities.

To satisfy her perpetual curiosity, Madame intrudes on the lesson and we soon learn the lady's name, particulars of her family, even to the detail about the brother working in Saudi Arabia.

'Do you think he might send us some special goods on request?' I find myself asking her. She would enquire, she says.

I leave the *pension* for the Café de la Paix to meet Engineer Ali Bakir.

'Every step is carefully laid out,' he says confidently. 'It's in the bag.' Good! So let's take the leap and make our earthly sojourn

worthwhile after all. 'I met Safeya Barakat at the Délices. Have
you really ditched her?'

'To hell with her!'

Looking shrewdly at me, he laughs. 'But have you really left her
for a . . .?'

'How can you believe her? Since when was she somebody
anyone could believe?'

For a moment or two he seems to assess me closely. Then he
says, 'I hope you understand that this deal of ours is the kind of
thing you don't talk about, not even to your wife or your own son.'

'God forgive you! What do you take me for?"

* * *

Wonderful! A look to flatter any male's ego. She didn't smile,
didn't bat an eyelid. She just suddenly turned her eyes away from
Zohra and her book and landed a look on me. As a rule I might
encounter scores of such eyes and never turn a hair. But hers
carried some kind of spark, transmitting a message that was quite
complete.

So I've changed my route and sit down behind the glass panes of
the Miramar Café, watching the clouds and waiting, not with any
clear end in view, not warmed by any touch of emotion, but out of
sheer curiosity born of boredom and despair, a simple craving for
an adventure of any kind. Actually, she isn't at all the kind of girl
that grabs me, but that look she gave me was as welcome as an
invitation to a picnic on an otherwise empty weekend.

She passes by the front of the café, her hands deep in the pockets
of her grey overcoat. I follow her at a distance, then at the Atheneus come up to her. She has bought some sweets and is standing there debating which way to go. I say hello and invite her to a
cup of tea. She says she's been thinking of sitting down for a while
in the tea-room, so we might as well. We drink our tea and eat two
pieces of pastry. Our conversation is cursory but not without
interest, in part because of the useful information I gather about
her family and her work. In any case it makes me ask for another
date, when we meet in the café at the Amir Cinema, then go in
together to see the film. It's up to me from then on to decide what
kind of affair it's going to be.

I don't find her worth a great deal of effort. And yet when she
invites me to meet her family, I accept. I realize that she's looking
for a husband and I weigh it all up cold-bloodedly—her salary and

what she makes out of private lessons. And always in my mind is the increasing hopelessness of my relationship with Zohra.

When I meet the family I find a new attraction: they own a fair-sized tenement house in Karmouz.[63] I find myself actually taking it all seriously, not out of love for the girl or greed for wealth—theirs is only moderate, after all—but simply to satisfy the longing I've had for a prosperous marriage. But what about Zohra? Is it conceivable that I could find consolation for having abandoned Zohra in marriage to a woman I don't love? Perhaps. But can I really fight down a passion so fixed, so deeply entrenched in my heart?

*　　*　　*

I had bought the paper and was turning away when Mahmoud made a signal to me to wait a little while he served another customer. When he'd finished, he turned to me.

'*Ustaz*, I'm going to propose to Zohra.'

To cover my dismay, I grinned at him. 'Congratulations! Have you settled it with her?'

'Almost.' He seemed very sanguine.

My heart beat painfully. 'What do you mean by "almost"?'

'Well, she's a regular customer, comes here every day. I haven't proposed to her in so many words, but I understand women pretty well.' I hated him. 'What do you think of her character, sir?'

'Very good. As a matter of fact.'

'Until I can meet her people, I'll try to speak for her through Madame.'

I wished him luck and walked away. I'd gone only two steps when he caught up with me. 'What do you know about her quarrel with her family?'

'Who told you about that?'

'Amer Bey, the old gentleman.'

'All I know is that she's extremely stubborn and proud.'

'Oh? Well, I know the answer to that one,' he boasted. Then he laughed.

When he did propose he was refused. I was delighted, but it added to my sense of guilt and responsibility. I was torn by love and anxiety, and for the time being Aleya's image seemed to recede and grow fainter in the background. It was with pleading tenderness that I took Zohra's wrists.

'Zohra! Save me! Let's go away at once,' I begged.

115

But she disengaged herself roughly. 'Stop that. I hate to hear it.'

It's no good, I thought. She loves me, but won't give in without marriage: and I love her, but cannot accept that bond. And both positions, hers and mine, have nothing to do with love that should annihilate mind and will.

Aleya's father, el-Sayyid Mohammed, invited me to lunch with them and I accepted. At the end of the week I invited the whole family to dinner at Pastoroudis'. After we had sat down in the restaurant, the weather changed; the wind whistled dismally and the rain came down in torrents. I tried to convince myself that Aleya was an excellent girl and that it would be a fine match. *She's good looking, very well dressed, educated, with a good salary. What more can you want? If she hadn't liked me . . . but why am I so reserved? She certainly loves me. If she wants a husband, she certainly wants a lover. What have I got out of love anyway? The heaven it promises is only an illusion.* Outside the storm raged, almost as if it intended to uproot the city. The sense of warmth and security indoors seemed only to be enhanced. *Now I've introduced myself to this respectable family, without any definite plans or sincere intentions. I haven't even got any money. I should let them know the situation, tell them about my commitments to my family—and leave it up to them.* The conversation soon led to the subject of 'marriage' in general.

'In my day,' said Aleya's father, 'we used to marry early and have the pleasure of seeing our children grow to manhood in our lifetime.'

Those were the days,' I said, shaking my head sadly. 'Our times are as hard as stone.'

He leaned towards me. 'A good man is a fortune in himself,' he whispered. 'Honest people should make things easy for him.'

*   *   *

His face was distorted with rage. I'd been only two steps from his stall when he'd noticed me and his whole expression had changed violently. Looking daggers, he muttered something sarcastic without bothering to give me the paper I took every day.

'Why didn't you tell me you were her lover?'

His impudence startled me. I shouted, 'You're out of your mind!'

'Coward!'

I lost my temper. I slapped his face with the back of my hand,

and he slapped me. Then we grappled blindly, punching each other until passers-by tore us apart and we separated trading insults and curses. For some time afterwards I walked without seeing where I was going, wondering who could have slipped that idea into his empty head.

A long time passed before I saw him again. I had gone into Panayoti's restaurant for a light supper, saw him sitting at the proprietor's place in front of the cash desk, and was on the point of going out again when he leapt up from his seat, embraced me, and kissed my head.[64] He insisted on serving me supper on the house, apologized for his past offence and informed me it was Hosni Allam who had told him such a lie.

*   *   *

'My dear, please don't let Zohra know anything about us.'

We were sitting at the Palma beside the Mahmoudiya Canala, enjoying the warmth of the sun. Her regular contact with Zohra worried me. Aleya knew nothing about Zohra's real motive for taking lessons and Zohra had no notion that her teacher had stolen her man.

'Why?' she asked, suspiciously.

'She's a terrible gossip. We don't want any gossip at this stage of our engagement.'

'But our engagement will be known sooner or later.'

I tried being blunt. 'Sometimes I think she has a special fancy for me.'

She smiled wanly. 'Maybe she has reasons for it.'

'All the lodgers tease her occasionally. I've done the same. That's all.'

Our relationship had developed considerably and Aleya had come to love me. I didn't care whether she believed me or not; I just wanted her to be on her guard with Zohra. Reason had finally got the better of love. It was up to me now to announce the engagement. But I still hesitated, putting it off under the pretext that I had to apply to my family and invite them down from the village to play their traditional role.

Every day my feelings towards Zohra became more painfully tense. I couldn't bear the thought of letting her down so shamefully. I burned with remorse for my treachery. *If only she would give in, I told myself, I'd be faithful forever.*

*   *   *

What's that? Thunder? An earthquake? Or a demonstration? Has anything fallen in my room? I put my head out from under the bedclothes. It was pitch-dark; and I was myself. *Yes, this is my bed, and this is my room at the Pension Miramar. But what's that? God, it's Zohra! She's calling for help!* I ran out and saw her by the nightlight struggling desperately with Hosny Allam.

I guessed the reason for the scene at once and tried to save her without too much scandal and without spoiling my relationship with Hosny. I laid my hand gently on his arm. 'Hosny.'

But he didn't hear me. I caught him by the shoulder and said aloud, 'Hosny, are you out of your mind?'

He shrugged me off violently, but I clutched him by both shoulders and said firmly, 'Go into the bathroom and stick your finger down your throat.'

He turned on me and hit me on the forehead. Mad with anger, I hit him back and we didn't stop until Madame came out. She treated the aggressor too leniently. I understood the old woman perfectly. *She was like me, hoping to get something out of his famous business project. The door is closed in my face now I thought, and she's ready to blame me for his sake.*

A few days later I caught sight of him leaving the Genevoise, at about one in the morning, in the company of Safeya Barakat, and I remembered the day he had taken her out of the *pension*. *They're birds of a feather, those two,* I thought, *impulsive dreamers. I suppose they'll live together on love and dreams.*

I had spent the evening at George's Bar with Ali Bakir and Rafat Amin. It was a clear night and we walked on the Corniche, braced by the wine and the weather. Rafat Amin's only subject, especially when he was drunk, was the Wafd. And Ali Bakir, I soon realized, hardly knew the difference between the Wafd and the National Sporting Club. Personally I don't care for politics, in spite of my considerable political activity. So when Rafat Amin went on and on about the Wafd in a thick drunken voice, I asked him ironically, 'Can't you tell when something is dead and buried?'

'Praise the Revolution all you like,' he roared in a voice that echoed through the deserted streets. 'I can't gainsay its overwhelming power. But I believe that when the Wafd died, the Egyptian masses died too.'

It was then that I saw Hosny and Safeya making for the Corniche, like two ambling bears. I pointed them out at a distance and said with a laugh, 'There are your Wafdist masses, mobilized, ready, prepared to carry their gallant struggle far on into the night.'

Before I left Ali Bakir whispered in my ear. 'We'll soon give the go-ahead.'

They were all asleep when I got back to the *pension*. I could see a light under Mansour Bahy's door. I knocked and went in. I had no motive for this late visit; it was the wine. He looked up at me in surprise. He was sitting in his armchair and I took a seat near him.

'Excuse me,' I said. 'I'm drunk.'

'Evidently.'

'I have failed in fact to make a friend of you.' I smiled apologetically. 'You're such an introvert.'

'It takes all sorts to make a world.' He was polite, but not encouraging.

'I suppose you're preoccupied with the problems of your own thinking?'

He replied enigmatically. 'My own thinking is the problem.'

'Blessed are we, the empty-headed.' I laughed.

'Oh come on. You're the centre of ceaseless mental activity.'

'Really?'

'Yes. Your political life, your revolutionary ideas. Your numerous conquests.'

I was struck by the last phrase, but I was too drunk to take it seriously. I understood I wasn't welcome, so I shook him by the hand and left.

* * *

When Zohra comes into my room with the tea-tray, I forget all my plans and give myself up to love. But her face is hard, pale and angry.

'Zohra, what's the matter?' I ask with concern.

'If I didn't know that God's wisdom was above everything, I'd lose my faith.'

'What's wrong? Is it some new trouble?'

'I saw the two of you with my own eyes.' She spits the words out contemptuously.

I know who she means and my heart falls. I ask desperately, 'You mean ...'

'The teacher,' she says with savage hatred. 'That whore, that man-hunter.'

119

I laugh. I have to, affecting the kind of careless laughter we use to face unjustified anger.

'If you mean your teacher, I just met her by chance and did her a courtesy.'

'Liar,' she cuts in savagely. 'It was *not* by chance. She told me about it today.'

'No!'

'The bitch admitted she'd been going out with you. Her parents weren't at all surprised. They were surprised at my asking questions.'

I am dumb, unable to say a word to appease her. She cries out in enraged disgust.

'Why does God make sneaks like you?'

I'm shattered, defeated. 'Zohra!' I beg from the depth of my despair. 'There's no reason to behave like this. I only turned to her in desperation. Please reconsider it, Zohra. We've got to get out of here.'

She doesn't seem to hear a word I say.

'What can I do? I have no claims on you. You filthy swine. To hell with you!' She spits in my face.

In spite of my shameful situation, I'm suddenly furious. I shout, 'Zohra!'—she spits at me again—'Get out of my sight, or I'll smash your head to bits.' I am blind with rage. She leaps at me, slapping my face with unbelievable strength. I shoot up out of my chair in fury and seize her wrist, but she tears away violently and slaps me again. Losing all control, I hit her savagely and she hits back more strongly than I could ever have imagined. Then Madame comes running in, protesting in outlandish gibberish, and takes Zohra away.

'It's none of your business!' I scream after her. 'I'll marry whomever I like. I'll marry Aleya.'

Mansour Bahy comes and takes me to his room. I can't remember afterwards how the conversation went, but I remember his impudence and I remember that I found myself involved in another fight. His behaviour came as a complete surprise to me. I hadn't suspected that he was in love with Zohra too. It explained his strange aloofness with me. Madame arrives on the scene and decides to make a scapegoat of me, the old whore. She says the *pension* has lost its peace since I came to stay, that I've turned it into a public market, with vulgar fighting and rioting.

'Find yourself another place to stay!' she says in a shrill voice.

I have nothing to stay for; out of obstinate pride, however, I insist on staying until the next day, since I've paid the rent in advance.

I go out and wander aimlessly in the streets under a cloudy sky, pregnant with rain. I look in the shop windows brilliant with New Year gifts and stare listlessly at old Santa Claus. Then I go to Pedro's to meet Ali Bakir.

'I hope you've taken care of the alibis,' he says. 'We start tomorrow at dawn.'

*   *   *

Early in the morning I go to work thinking, 'The dawn is over; the die is cast.' I am tense, impatient for news. I ring the plant and ask for Ali Bakir, but they tell me he's on his morning round. Good. Everything has gone according to plan and he's doing his routine work as usual. Too excited to work, I leave the office early. As I pass by Broadcasting House, I see Mansour and a pretty girl going out together. *Who can it be? His fiancée? His mistress? Will Zohra find herself on the shelf a second time?* At the thought of Zohra I am depressed, which makes me realize that I'm not cured of love for her yet. It's been the only true emotion that ever beat in my wayward heart.

I pay a visit to Aleya Mohammed and her family, who give me a very cool welcome. I'd intended to invent a few lies, but her father bursts out angrily.

'Imagine a housemaid taking us to task like that!'

It's lunchtime, but no one asks me to stay and I leave their flat without any hope of putting things right. Not that I really care. *In a few hours I'll be rich and sure to find a splendid wife.* I have lunch at Panayoti's—Abu el Abbas's now—then move on to Ali Bakir's house, but he isn't at home and by the time I get to the *pension* I am frantic for news. I pack my suitcase and take it to the entrance hall. From there I ring Ali Bakir and when I hear his voice over the receiver I am immensely relieved.

'Hello.'

'This is Sarhan. Greetings. How are things?'

'Everything's fine. I haven't talked with the driver yet.'

'When do we know?'

'Let's meet at eight o'clock, at the Swan.'

I leave the Pension Miramar and check in at the Pension Eva. Aimless after that, I wander from one café to another, drinking all the time, throwing my money away, drowning my anxiety and the pain of my love-tormented heart in drink, and vowing that my family will enjoy prosperity they've never dreamt of since my father died. A little before eight I arrive at the Swan. I am annoyed to run into Tolba Marzuq at the entrance, but I shake his hand, pretending I'm glad to see him.

'What brings you here?' he says.

'A date.'

'Well. Let me buy you a drink. We'll sit together until your friend comes.' We sit in the winter lounge. 'Cognac?' he asks me, his hollow voice reverberating in his jowls. I am drunk already, but thirsty for more. We drink, talking, laughing.

'Do you think they'd let me go to Kuwait to visit my daughter?' he suddenly asks.

'I expect so. Do you want to make a new start?'

'No. But my son-in-law— he's also my nephew—has become very rich.'

'You're probably thinking of emigrating.'

There is a cautious look in his eyes, 'No. I just want to see my daughter.'

I draw my head near his. 'Shall I tell you something that should comfort you?'

'What's that?'

'Some people don't like the Revolution. But look at it this way: what other system could we have in its place? If you think clearly, you'll realize that it has to be either the Communists or the Muslim Brotherhood. Which of those lots would you prefer to the Revolution?'

'Neither,' he replies hastily.

I smile in triumph. 'Exactly. Let that be your comfort.'

It is time. But Ali Bakir has not shown up. I wait in agony for another half hour, then I telephone his flat, but get no answer. He's probably on his way. *So what's keeping him? Can't he understand what this delay is doing to me?*

Tolba Marzuq looks at his watch. 'It's time for me to go.' He shakes me by the hand and leaves.

I cannot stop drinking. Finally a waiter calls me to the telephone. I run to the booth and take up the receiver, my heart thumping.

'Hello! Ali, why haven't you come?'

'Listen, Sarhan, it's gone badly wrong.'

His words are all mixed up with the alcohol blurring my brain, everything seems to be spinning around me.

'What's that you're saying?'

'We're lost!'

'But how? Tell me everything.'

'What difference does it make? The driver wanted the whole lot for himself. They got him and he's going to give everything away. He's probably done it already.'

'What do we do? What are you going to do?' My mouth has gone dry.

'We're finished. I'm going to do what the devil tells me.'

He rings off.

I'm trembling, shaking so badly that I can hardly stay on my feet. I think of running away, but the waiter is watching me. I go back to the table. But I can't sit down. I drink off what's left in my glass, pay my bill and walk out. But terror—suffocating, hopeless—is closing in on me. I can't fight it. I head for the bar, order a whole bottle and find myself drinking madly, while the barman watches in alarm, glass after glass, gulping it down without a pause or a word or a look around me. Then I'm looking up at him.

'A razor, please.'

The barman smiles, but does not move.

I say it again. 'A razor, please!'

He hesitates a little, but when he sees the look in my face he calls a waiter, who comes back from somewhere with a used blade. Thanks. I put it in my pocket. Now I'm turning away from the bar and walking out towards the front door, I'm reeling. Not from drunkenness. From desperation. Haste. I'm crossing the road, and I wish I had the strength left in me to run.

I have no hope. No hope.

5. AMER WAGDI

My peace had been destroyed by all these incidents. I had taken asylum in Mariana's *pension* hoping to live quietly in my old age and to find consolation in my memories for the unbearably cruel disappointment of the last years of my career. It had not occurred to me that it would turn into an arena of brutal conflict, ending with violence and even murder.

When a little energy had welled up in me again, I joined Mariana and Tolba Marzuq for our usual gathering in the hall. I wished to see Zohra, but Mariana's hysterics and Tolba's scowls prohibited it. I didn't wish to bring her into such an atmosphere which would be intensified by her woes and would not respect them. I understood that Hosny Allam had gone out at his usual hour. He had been upset by the terrible news for a while, but soon seemed to forget it altogether. Mansour Bahy, on the other hand, behaving quite unlike his usual self, was still in bed asleep.

'Here's a miserable ending to the year,' complained Mariana. 'I wonder what the New Year has in store for us.'

'A lot of trouble, no doubt!' said Tolba irritably.

'As long as we're not to blame . . .' I muttered.

He snapped, 'You're protected by your old age.'

We heard Mansour's door open; he was on his way to the bathroom. Half an hour later he went back to his room. A little after that he came out from behind the screen, his eyes clouded. Madame told him his breakfast was ready, but he refused it with a shake of his head, not saying a word. It upset us all to see him in this condition. Madame was the first to speak.

'Won't you sit down, Monsieur Mansour? Are you all right?'

'Quite all right.' He still stood. 'I've overslept, that's all.'

Madame pointed to the newspaper spread out on the sofa.

'Haven't you heard the news?' He didn't seem interested. 'Sarhan el-Beheiry was found dead on the road to the Palma.'

He gazed into her eyes, showing no surprise or alarm, just staring at her, as if he had not heard or did not understand. Or perhaps he was more seriously ill than we had imagined. Mariana offered him the paper. He looked at it blankly for a while, then read in silence. We were all watching him. Then he looked up.

'Yes, he was found dead—murdered.'

'Do sit down,' I said. 'You're tired.'

'I'm all right,' he replied coldly, probably not fully conscious of what he was saying.

'You can see we're rather worried,' remarked Mariana.

He looked from one face to another.

'Why?'

'Well, we're afraid the police will come. It will be very upsetting.'

'They won't come.'

'But the police, don't you know . . .' began Tolba Marzuq.

'I killed Sarhan el-Beheiry,' said Mansour. Then, before we had understood what he said, he walked to the door, opened it, and looked back at us. 'I'm going to the police myself.'

He closed the door behind him. We looked at one another in amazement and for a moment were all struck dumb.

'He's mad,' said Mariana, panic-stricken.

'No, he's sick,' I said.

'Maybe he did kill him,' said Tolba Marzuq after a pause.

'That timid, well-behaved young man?'

'He's certainly sick,' I said, feeling sorry for the boy.

'But why should he kill him?' wondered Mariana.

'Why should he confess that he did it?' wondered Tolba in his turn.

'I'll never forget his face,' said Mariana. 'Something has touched his brain.'

Tolba went on with his theorizing. 'He was the last one to fight with Sarhan.'

I protested that everyone had fought with him.

'There lies the cause,' he said, pointing to Zohra's room.

I began to be angry. 'But he's the only one who hasn't shown any special interest in her.'

'That doesn't necessarily mean that he wasn't in love with her, or that he didn't wish to take revenge on a rival.'

'My dear sir, Sarhan left her.'

'Yes, he left her. But he took her heart and her honour.'

'Do shut up. Don't accuse people like that.'

'Will he really go to the police?' said Mariana.

We went on talking heatedly until we were exhausted and finally I called a halt.

'That's enough,' I said. 'We'll submit to what Providence decrees.'

*　　*　　*

> *Or as darkness on a vast, abysmal sea.*
> *There covereth him a wave, above which is a wave, above which is a cloud.*
> *Layer upon layer of darkness.*
> *When he holdeth out his hand he scarce can see it.*
> *And he for whom Allah hath not appointed light, for him there is no light.*
>
> *Hast thou not seen that Allah. He it is Whom all are in the heavens and the earth praise, and the birds in their flight? Of each He knoweth verily the worship and the praise: and Allah is aware of what they do.*
>
> *And unto Allah belongeth the sovereignty of the heavens and unto Allah is the journeying.*[65]

My eyes soon grew tired of reading. As I left my room it struck four. Mariana was writing in the hall.

'It's the first time I've spent such a depressing New Year's Eve,' she said. 'It's like a funeral.'

'No more of that, please,' said Tolba Marzuq.

'It's like a curse on the place,' she went on angrily. 'Zohra must go. She'll have to earn her living somewhere else.'

I felt stabbed. 'But Mariana, what's she done? She's just unlucky. It's not her fault. She's turned to you in her trouble.'

'She's brought bad luck with her.'

'Why don't *we* celebrate the New Year?' said Tolba, snapping his fingers as if he'd found a bright idea.

'*We?*' I said. 'How ridiculous!'

But he ignored me.

'Get ready, my dear,' he said to Mariana. 'We'll go out together as we planned.'

'But my nerves, Monsieur Tolba, my nerves . . .'

'That's why I'm taking you out.'

And as far as they were concerned, everything was suddenly transformed.

Hosny Allam came in and announced his intention of moving out of the *pension*. When we told him about Mansour Bahy's strange confession, he was genuinely surprised. He talked it over for a while, then shrugged his broad shoulders, went and packed his suitcase, said goodbye, and left.

'We're back on our own, as we started,' I commented sadly when I saw him go.

Tolba said merrily, 'Thank God for that!'

And suddenly they were bubbling with energy and excitement and there were no traces of anxiety left. Mariana was decked out as she would have been in the old days. She wore a dark blue evening gown that set off the whiteness of her skin, a black coat with a real fur collar and gilded shoes; and she had put on diamond earrings and a string of pearls. Covering the signs of age with *maquillage,* she seemed to have reverted to the days of her famous beauty. As she stood in the hall, theatrically posed, we looked at each other. And she laughed with joy, like a young girl.

'I'll wait for you,' she said to Tolba as she went out, 'at the hairdresser's.'

* * *

I was all by myself, with nothing to keep me company but the howling of the wind. I called for Zohra. I had to call her three times before she finally appeared from behind the screen. She stood there, looking inexpressibly sad and broken, until it seemed to me as if she had actually become bent and shrunken. I pointed to the sofa. Without a word she crossed the room and sat down, under the statue of the Madonna. She folded her arms and looked down at the floor. My heart was so filled with tenderness and compassion for her that tears, too feeble at this late period in my life to give me the relief of weeping, sprang to my eyes.

'Why do you sit there alone, as if you were without friends? Listen. I'm an old man, very old, as you see. I stumbled in my life three or four times. When that happened, I would cry "It's all over!" and wish I could kill myself. But here I am, as you see, at an age that very few live to. And all that's left of those terrible times of despair are vague memories, without odour, taste or significance. They might have happened to someone else.'

She listened without response.

'Let's leave grief to time, which wears away iron and stone. You must think of your future. The truth is, Madame doesn't want you to stay.'

'I don't care!'

'What are your plans for the future?'

'Just what they were,' she said, looking at the floor. 'Until I get what I want.'

I sensed a strength of will in her that reassured me. 'It's right that you should go on with your plan of learning a profession. But how will you live?'

'I'm offered work at every turn.' She spoke with both confidence and defiance.

'What about your village?' I said gently, trying to be persuasive. 'Won't you consider going home?'

'No. They don't think well of me.'

'What about Mahmoud Abu el Abbas?' I was almost begging her. 'He has his faults, but you're strong. You could certainly reform him.'

'He's no better than anyone at home.'

I gave up. 'I'd so like to see you happy and well, Zohra.' I sighed. 'I'm very fond of you and I know you like me. And I hope you'll come to me if you're ever in trouble or need.' She looked at me with affectionate gratitude. 'However painful your past experience has been life will still be the same. You'll still go on looking for the one man who can make you happy.' She lowered her head and sighed. 'And you will find the man who is worthy of you. He's there now, somewhere. Perhaps he's been waiting for the right happy moment to meet you.'

She murmured something I couldn't understand, but I had the feeling that what she had said was right.

'Life is still good,' I said. 'And it will always be so.'

We sat together for a while, between harmony and silence. After some time, she excused herself and went to her room.

I had fallen asleep in my chair and woke up at the sound of the door opening. Mariana and Tolba came in singing. They were drunk. Tolba shouted, 'What are you doing up so late, old man?'

'What's the time?' I asked, yawning, rather startled.

'We are two hours into the New Year,' said Mariana in a blurred, intoxicated voice. The man pulled her after him to his room, kissing her, and she followed after a half-hearted show of resistance. The door closed behind them. I sat looking at it as if in a dream.

*   *   *

Madame did not come to the table and after setting breakfast Zohra left Tolba and me alone. He had a hangover.

'Lovely morning,' I said, pulling his leg. 'And congratulations.'

He ignored me for some time, then murmured, 'It's your evil eye!' But he soon burst out laughing. 'It was such a flop, a double fiasco—ludicrous and humiliating at the same time.'

I pretended not to understand.

'You know what I mean, you old fox!'

'Mariana?'

He could not help laughing again. 'We tried everything you could imagine. In vain. When she took off her clothes she looked like a wax mummy. "What in the world have we sunk to now?" I said to myself.'

'You must have beeen out of your mind.'

'Then she had a kidney attack. Started crying, if you can imagine. Said I was mutilating her!'

After breakfast he followed me into my room and sat down facing me.

'I think I'll go to Kuwait soon. Our departed friend prophesied I would.'

'Departed friend?'

'Sarhan el-Beheiry.' He gave a short laugh. 'He tried to reconcile me to the Revolution with the most curious argument. He assured me that the only alternatives to the Revolution were either the Communists or the Brothers. And he thought he'd covered it all!'

I could not see that he hadn't. 'But that's the truth.'

'There *is* a third alternative,' he said mockingly.

'What's that?'

'America.'

'You want the United States to govern us?'

'Through a moderate right wing.' He mused. 'Why not?'

I'd had enough of Tolba's dreams.

'Go to Kuwait, before you lose your mind completely!'

*   *   *

The papers have carried news of the crime—strange, contradictory news. Mansour Bahy confessed to having committed the murder, but could not convince anyone as to his motives. He said he had killed Sarhan because in his opinion Sarhan deserved such a punishment. Why had he deserved it? Because of conduct and qualities bad in themselves, but by no means peculiar to Sarhan. Then why had Mansour chosen him? By mere chance; he might have picked someone else. Those were his answers. Who would have been convinced by such talk? Could the boy be really deranged or was he only pretending?

The post-mortem report stated the cause of death to be a razor cut across the arteries of the left wrist, not a beating with a shoe, as the alleged murderer had claimed. It appeared that most probably it had been a suicide. Then, when the relationship between the victim and the incident of the lorry of stolen yarn came out, the hypothesis of suicide was confirmed.

We wonder what sentence Mansour will get. He will probably be released soon to pick up his life again. But with what heart? Or what reason? 'He's an excellent young man,' I think sadly, 'but he suffers from some secret malady of which he must be cured.'

And then there's Zohra, looking, except for a touch of sadness, just as she did when I first saw her. These days that have passed have given her more depth than all the preceding years of her life. I take the cup from her, disguising my old man's heavy-heartedness with a smile.

She says casually, 'I'm leaving tomorrow morning.'

I have tried to persuade Madame to keep her, but she has refused. For her part, Zohra has told me that she wouldn't stay even if Madame changed her mind. 'I am going to a better place,' she says— and believes it.

'God bless you!'

She gives me a tender smile. 'And I shall never forget you as long as I live.'

I motion to her to bring her face nearer to me and kiss her on both cheeks. 'Thank you, Zohra.'

Then I whisper in her ear.

'Remember that you haven't wasted your time here. If you've come to know what is not good for you, you may also think of it all as having been a sort of magical way of finding out what is truly good for you.'

And as often happens, when my heart is too full, I turn to the Sura of the Beneficent, and recite:

The Beneficent
Hath made known the Koran.
He hath created man.
He hath taught him utterance.
The sun and the moon are made punctual.
The stars and the trees adore.
And the sky He hath uplifted; and He hath set the measure,
That ye exceed not the measure,
But observe the measure strictly, nor fall short thereof.
And the earth hath He appointed for His creatures.
Wherein are fruit and sheathed palm trees,
Husked grain and scented herb.
Which is it, of the favours of your Lord, that ye deny?[266]

NOTES

1. *Lady of the Dew.* Literally, 'beautiful dew drop', an epithet identified with Princess Qatr el-Nada (Beautiful Dew Drop), the pampered daughter of Sultan Khumaraweyh ibn Ahmed ibn Tulun (864–905). Khumaraweyh's court was renowned for its luxury—the Sultan took his siesta in a garden of gold and silver fruit trees, floating at the centre of a pool of quicksilver on a leather air-mattress tethered by silver cords to silver mooring-posts, guarded by a blue-eyed lion—and Qatr el-Nada's wedding journey from the Egyptian capital to Baghdad as the bride of the Caliph was an event of dazzling splendour, unparalleled until the heyday of the Fatimids, a century or so later.

2. *The massive old building . . . tongue of land . . . shotguns cracking incessantly.* The actual approximate site of the author's imagined building, with the fictional Pension Miramar on its fourth floor and a fictional Café Miramar on the groundfloor, is occupied at present by a busy place of entertainment (*cf.* the fictional Genevoise) that specializes in the diversions traditionally enjoyed by visiting seamen and bears (no doubt by coincidence) the same name as the novel. The nearby tongue of land is the Silsila (the Chain), a breakwater protecting the eastern entrance to the Eastern Harbour. At the seaward tip of the Silsila stands the Tiro Club, which used to offer its customers not only food and drink, but also trap-shooting over the water.

3. *Anfushi.* Amer Wagdi is reminded by Mariana's laugh of the district where he was born, a fishing community at the seaward extremity of the peninsula separating the Eastern and Western Harbours, where his father was keeper of the major mosque. See Notes 9 and 23.

4. *the Pasha.* A fictional character based in part upon the historic character of Saad Pasha Zaghloul (1860–1927), the great nationalist statesman, Minister of Education (1910), Minister of Justice (1912), founder of the Wafd, leader of the 1919 Revolution (see Note 8), and Prime Minister (1924–1927). See Notes 8, 16, 26. Despite retrospective attacks on his character from both the right and the left, Saad's memory remains revered throughout Egypt. Among many very human traits was the fact that he could not differentiate in speech between Arabic consonants *qaf* and *kaf*, which made possible a confusion between *qalb* (heart) and *kalb* (dog), represented here by 'core' and 'cur'. With important exceptions, through which Mahfouz suggests the subsequent moral

decline of the Wafd, the words attributed throughout the novel to the Pasha could have been spoken by Saad.

5. *the Trianon.* A fashionable tea-room near the Cecil Hotel (see Note 11) formerly the meeting place of officials and politicians.

6. *your people.* Amer Wagdi refers, of course, not just to Mariana's family or friends but to the Greeks of Alexandria, the ethnic descendants of its founders, most of whom left the country after the July Revolution.

7. *Umm Kulthum.* The most famous and most adored of Egypt's female singers (1899–1975), whose concerts on the first Thursday of each winter month between 1937 and the nineteen-seventies were broadcast from Cairo over all the Arab world.

8. *The first revolution ... the second ... the Revolution of 1919.* Using the war against the Central Powers as their excuse, the British had deposed the Khedive Abbas Hilmy in 1914 and established a Protectorate, effectively suspending meanwhile the parliamentary powers of the Legislative Assembly. Immediately after the Armistice a delegation (in Arabic, *wafd*) led by Saad Zaghloul approached the British authorities to demand complete independence. Rebuffed in Cairo and refused permission to travel to London or Paris, where the Egyptian case might, they hoped, have been argued more effectively, the Wafd then organized a campaign for support that led to the arrest and deportation of Saad and three other notables. Demonstrations of protest over this event broke out on 9 March 1919; and on 10 and 11 March—events that Amer Wagdi participated in and remembers well—they spread to al-Azhar (see Note 9), where British soldiers killed or wounded a number of students. Almost instantly the whole country rose. More than 800 Egyptians were killed during the next three weeks, at the end of which the British capitulated on the issue of Saad's arrest. After three more years of continual struggle, Whitehall allowed the establishment of a monarchy under Fuad I and with it a limited amount of sovereignty, though the Occupation itself was in effect to continue for another thirty years, during which the Wafd became the dominant political party in Egypt. Like Amer Wagdi, however, the old Wafd has no heirs. The second revolution, the July Revolution led by Gamal Abdel Nasser in 1952, put an end to the monarchy and the Wafd as well as the Occupation.

9. *Khan Gaafar ... Khan el Khalili ... the Club ... the turban ... al-Azhar.* Khan Gaafar is a street in the heart of the Gamaliya, the vivid mediaeval quarter where Mahfouz himself (like the Khedive Ismail) was born, and of which in his famous Trilogy he has made the most extensive artistic record. A large portion of the Gamaliya is covered by the Khan el Khalili, a bazaar area since the fourteenth century and well known to tourists as 'the Mouski', a name properly applied to an adjacent area in the neighbouring district of the Ghuriya. The Club was a cinema (al-Club al-Misry) that flourished in the Gamaliya from the First World War onward; like Feshawi's, a nine-hundred-year-old coffee-house recently half-demolished to make room for a parking lot, it was one of the centres of the cultural florescence that took place in the Gamaliya

during the Twenties and Thirties, when the district was still essentially middle-class, as exemplified in Amer Wagdi's prospective father-in-law. The turban of the prospective father-in-law indicates in this instance a sheikh trained at al-Azhar (The Resplendent), Cairo's thousand-year-old teaching mosque which stands in the Ghuriya, a stone's throw away from Khan Gaafar, and is now a university, the international centre of Islamic learning. As keeper of the Mosque of Sidi Abu el-Abbas el-Morsy, the principal sea-front mosque of Alexandria, Amer Wagdi's father would also presumably have been Azhar-trained. (Sidi Abu el-Abbas el-Morsy, who died in the fourteenth century, is the patron saint, as it were, of Alexandria's sailors and fishermen; the Mosque is an eighteenth-century Turkish-style building that replaces an earlier structure and overlooks the Eastern Harbour from Anfushi. (See Note 3.) The reason for Amer Wagdi's expulsion from al-Azhar is not clear but it very likely involved 'the least thing'. Taha Hussein, whose classic *Stream of Days* (1939) is a description of student life at al-Azhar during precisely the same era when Amer Wagdi must have been there (*circa* 1905), tells us that the order for his own expulsion arose from a private remark to the effect that a single ambiguous statement ascribed to a general who died in 714 might conceivably be insufficient to convict that general posthumously of heresy. Reinstated through the influence of two powerful politicians, one of whom declared that he had committed a 'sin', Taha Hussein later left al-Azhar and the world of the turban for what he calls 'the world of the tarboosh', the world of secular thought and religious reform, symbolized in the then-modernist headgear that had been introduced from Turkey and that only three decades later, after the July Revolution, would come to be associated with reactionary old gentlemen like Tolba Marzuq. Saad Zaghloul himself, Amer Wagdi's 'master', made the same transition at an earlier date.

10. *Ahmed Shafiq . . . Sharia Mohamed Aly.* Ahmed Shafiq (1860–1940) chronicled the history of the Wafd. Sheikh Aly Mahmoud (1902–1949) was famous as the developer of a style of Koranic recitation and Zakariya Ahmad (1890–1961) was a renowned composer. Both were identified with the cultural life of the Gamaliya. Sayed Darwish (1893–1923), the finest singer of modern Egypt before Umm Kulthum (see Note 7), has given his name to the foremost of Cairo's concert halls and his songs are not only sung with undiminished success but have recently been stunningly adapted to contemporary tastes by Mohamed Nuh. The People's Party and the Nationalist Party were rivals of the Wafd. The Muslim Brotherhood, which like the Communist Party was banned after the July Revolution, espoused the idea of a state founded on theocratic principles. Sharia Mohammad Aly (*Sharia* means 'street') built by the Khedive Ismail (*regnavit* 1863–1879) in imitation of the Rue de Rivoli and named for his despotic grandfather, leads from Ezbekiya, the site of the Cairo Opera House (mysteriously destroyed by fire in 1971), to the foot of the Citadel (see Note 33) and continues to be identified with musicians, dancers, and women of negotiable virtue. More especially identified with the latter was an area spreading a kilometre or so to the north and east of Ezbekiya known as the Wasa'a (the Open Land) where both local and imported services were formerly available in accommodation ranging from luxurious licenced houses to one-room hovels (see Note 32).

11. *the Atheneus, Pastoroudis', and the Antoniadis . . . the Cecil and the Windsor.* The Atheneus and Pastoroudis' are Greek restaurants. The Antoniadis is a park near the Mahmoudiya Canal (see Note 17). The Cecil and the Windsor were the leading hotels in Alexandria and had the status of institutions.

12. *the Sura of the Beneficent.* Al-Surat el-Rahman, Koran LV. (Pickthal translation, George Allen & Unwin.)

13. *Under-secretary of State for the Ministry of Mortmain Endowments.* Not without symbolic significance in the context of the novel, this post was formerly one of the most lucrative and powerful in the Egyptian government, since it involved administering, as a 'government within a government', the funds and property bequeathed by the Faithful to Islam, accounting for an enormous amount of capital, especially in the form of urban real-estate. Tolba Marzuq's character resembles in part that of one of the actual early Under-secretaries in this ministry, where Naguib Mahfouz himself was employed for several years.

14. *feddans.* A *feddan* is very nearly equivalent to an acre. At the time covered by the novel, legal land reforms instituted under the Nasser regime had reduced holdings by individuals first to two hundred, then to a hundred *feddans*, and they were later to be cut further, with compensation to the former owners. Many holdings were seized outright, however, along with houses, flats, cars, bank accounts, jewellery, furs, books, furniture, and other personal property, in actions that were described as sequestrations and have since been declared illegal. It should be understood that Tolba Marzuq's thousand *feddans* represented first-class agricultural land in a country where the *per capita* share of cultivable land was half an acre and is now two-tenths of an acre, and that such a holding would have been quite sufficient to maintain a millionaire. Land reforms would have reduced it to a hundred *feddans*, but apparently everything Tolba possessed has been placed under sequestration, including even this legal post-reform acreage.

15. *February Fourth.* On 4 February 1942, in the midst of the Second World War, the British drew up a tank battalion in front of Abdine Palace and forcibly installed a Wafd ministry that was presumed to be pro-Allied in its sympathies, thus reducing the Egyptian government openly to puppet status, damaging the moral prestige of the Wafd itself—the party originally identified with constitutionalism and nationalist aspirations—virtually beyond restitution, and laying the ground for the July Revolution ten years later. It is significant that Amer Wagdi, with his humane, high-minded, old-fashioned patriotism, should have abandoned—or been abandoned by—Egyptian politics.

16. *Saad Zaghloul.* See Notes 4 and 8.

17. *the Palma . . . the Mahmoudiya Canal.* The Palma is a tea-garden situated rather remotely from the centre of the city on the Mahmoudiya Canal, which links Alexandria with the Nile and defines the southern and western edges of the city proper.

18. *melaya . . . Sharia Mohammad Aly.* The *melaya* is the black shawl or drapery

traditionally used by Egyptian women as an outer garment or overcoat. For the significance of Sharia Mohammad Aly, see Note 10.

19. *Iblis.* The Koranic name of Satan. See Note 9, on *the turban*.

20. *the Prophet's Birth . . . the Dimirdashiyya.* The birthday of the Prophet is celebrated as a holiday in most Moslem countries. In Cairo a notable part of the celebration is a procession of the Sufi sects, one of the best endowed of which was the Dimirdashiyya, headed by a pasha of the Dimirdash family. Amer Wagdi's remarks reflect the opinion that this sect nurtured collaborationist tendencies.

21. *fellaha.* A farm-woman or peasant.

22. *Beheira.* The agricultural province adjoining Alexandria famous for its onions and other market produce.

23. *I kissed . . . with me.* 'She' is Amer Wagdi's widowed mother, living alone at Anfushi. See Note 3.

24. *gallabiyya.* The typical long cotton gown of Egypt, made fashionable recently in the West as a 'caftan'.

25. *Bargawan, Darb al Ahmar . . . Sidi Abu el Su'ud.* Bargawan, named for a tenth-century vizier, is in the neighbourhood of the Gamaliya. The Darb al Ahmar quarter takes its name from its major street, which is lined with fourteenth-century buildings and runs north-easterly from the Gate of the Vizier at the Citadel (see Note 33) to Bab Zuweila, the southern gate of the Fatimid royal enclosure in which the districts of the Gamaliya and the Ghuriya lie and for which the whole of Cairo is named. The shrine of Sidi Abu el Su'ud stands in Fustat, at the southern outskirts of modern Cairo, on what is now Sharia Salah Salem.

26. *Minister of Justice . . . effendi . . . Circassians.* See Note 5 on *the Pasha.* The conversation recorded here takes place before the Pasha had been elevated to that rank. As used in Egypt the Turkish title *effendi* (master) was freely applied as a mode of address to the clerical class and is now virtually equivalent to 'sir' or 'mister'. *Pasha* or *bey*, titles bestowed before 1914 by the Ottoman Sultan, came to signify wealth and social status rather than simply political power. From the Mameluke period until after 1919 the ruling class in Egypt, the class of the *pashas* and *beys*, was largely Turco-Circassian in origin. Turkish remained the court language until the accession of Farouk—whose first language was English—in 1936.

27. *Tanta.* A city in the Delta between Cairo and Alexandria, capital of the province of Gharbiyya.

28. *Liberation Organization . . . Company Board.* The Organizations listed by Sarhan are all parts of the apparatus set up by the July Revolution. See Note 55.

29. *1919, that bloody uprising.* The uprising following Saad's arrest. See Note 8.

30. *Bismillah . . . inheritors.* Koran XXVIII. 1–6 (The Sura of the Narration).

31. *My dear Pasha . . . Kasr el Nil Barracks.* The conversation here takes a symbolic turn to define the Pasha's (and the Wafd's) later character as opposed to the ideals for which Saad Zaghloul and the original Wafd had stood. The Agricultural Credit Bank was founded four years after Saad Zaghloul's death, reputedly with the aim of ruining Wafdist landowners, and still exists. The Kasr el Nil Barracks do not. Reserved by the British for the use of Guards regiments and therefore, not surprisingly, occupying the most luxurious site in Cairo (though also notoriously vermin-ridden), they have been replaced by Midan el-Tahrir (Liberation Square), the Arab League and Arab Socialist Union Secretariats, and the Nile Hilton Hotel.

32. *He clutched . . . officer's whore.* Amer Bey recalls a famous police episode of some forty years earlier, the sentencing of the notorious Ibrahim el-Gharby, the King of the Wasa'a (see Note 10)—an enormously obese Nubian transvestite who controlled the entire Cairene traffic in women during the second decade of the century—who amassed not only a fortune but also considerable social and political influence, was exiled to the country, and later died in prison, leaving his inheritance to a younger and more brutal generation. The political overtones behind this reminiscence should not be missed.

33. *Sault's, Groppi's, Alf Leila, and Lipton Gardens . . . the Citadel.* Sault's, Groppi's, and Lipton Gardens were tea-gardens in the area between Shepheard's Hotel (burned in 1952) and the Kasr el Nil Barracks (see Note 31). Groppi's still exists; the others have disappeared as the area has changed its character. The Citadel is a complex of buildings that dates back in its origins to Saladin. Overlooking Cairo from the Moqattam Hills east of the Nile, it has served as headquarters for military rule intermittently from that time down to the present. The nineteenth-century Turkish mosque that surmounts it contributes a picturesque if rather spurious 'oriental' highlight to the Cairo skyline; the small palace nearby was burned in 1972.

34. *Everyone . . . deny?* Koran LV. 25–27 (The Sura of the Beneficent). These verses have frequently been said to summarize the Arab view of what the West calls 'history' and are often quoted—being inscribed, for example, on the tomb in Cairo of one of the Abassid Caliphs, the sixth in that long line of luxuriously maintained but impotent figureheads.

35. *Ferekeeko.* A slang nomen of no certain lexical origin, modish among the alienated young of the early nineteen-sixties, approximately equivalent to *man* in 'Man, dig that!' or 'Watch your head, man!' An index to both period and social class the word is so distant from colloquial, classical, or literary Arabic as to suggest in itself a certain amount of conscious social rebellion.

36. *progeny of whores . . . feddans . . . Miss Blue-Eyes.* The possession of a hundred *feddans* (see Note 14) would suffice in itself to define Hosni's social position, for in an Egyptian context they could only represent the remains of a larger holding

reduced in the course of the July Revolution's land reforms. They would also suffice to keep him living comfortably. His own remarks, as well as his cousin Mervat's blue eyes and Turkish name, point to the fact that Hosni, like Tolba Marzuq, belongs to the remnants of the Turco-Circassian elite (see Note 26), many of whom traced their descent from Circassian concubines, girls who were either purchased or acquired as gifts and who were frequently passed on, slightly used, to friends, colleagues or clients of the original husband or owner.

37. *fort of Sultan Qaitbay ... giant stone jetty-arm.* Like Amer Wagdi, Hosny Allam looks out over the Eastern Harbour, which the Corniche, sweeping along the shore from right to left, shapes into a crescent that terminates two kilometres away across the harbour at Anfushi in a little peninsula surmounted by the fort of Sultan Qaitbay (d. 1495), situated on the site of the ancient Pharos. Near at hand to the right and running out perpendicular to the Corniche, almost closing the arc of the crescent, is the breakwater of the Silsila. (See Note 2.)

38. *the Revolutionary Charter.* Promulgated in February 1962, the Charter described 'the socialist situation' as 'inevitable' and defined the Arab Socialist Union as the major political instrument for guiding the Revolution into such a situation. (See Note 55.)

39. *Dream-Boy Beheiry.* Hosny puns on Sarhan's name, which means 'dreamer', and suggests both the strength of his charm and the weakness of his moral vision.

40. *nargileh.* The hubble-bubble or water pipe.

41. *Mazarita, Chatby, Ibrahimiya ... Siyouf ... the boulevard to Abu Qir.* The Pension Miramar stands in Mazarita, just within the Eastern Harbour. Immediately to the east, outside the harbour along the Corniche, is the district of Chatby; beyond lie Ibrahimiya, the Sporting Club district, Cleopatra, Camp de César, Sidi Gaber, and Siyouf.

42. *Omar Khayyam.* An Alexandrian restaurant.

43. *Qalawoon, the Doddering Sultan.* One of the ablest, most successful and long-lived (1220–1290) of the notoriously short-lived Mameluke Sultans, founder of a hospital that has served the Gamaliya continuously down to the present time, Qalawoon died while on his way at the age of seventy to lead a siege against Acre. His name is Mongol in origin and may have an absurd ring in Arabic, which the editors have tried to suggest in their transliteration, but Hosny's allusion in referring to Amer Wagdi by the name is intended as ironic on other grounds which the editors have attempted to clarify with the epithet 'Doddering Sultan'. There is an additional irony, however, given Amer Wagdi's lamented childlessness, in that Qalawoon founded a dynasty lasting nearly a hundred years.

44. *the portrait.* A portrait of Gamal Abdel Nasser (1918–1970) leader of the July Revolution.

45. *Cleopatra.* See Note 41.

46. *I've seen you together.* A piquant allusion on Hosny's part to a song popular in the early nineteen-sixties that began: 'Don't lie to me—I've seen you together.'

47. *Qaitbay . . . Abu Qir . . . Siyouf . . . Chatby . . . Sidi Gaber.* (See Note 41.)

48. *Pam Pam.* A restaurant and nightclub near the Corniche.

49. *Moharrem Bey.* An inland district.

50. *our lord Omar.* The second of the four Orthodox Caliphs who immediately succeeded the Prophet as heads of Islam, renowned for his piety, abstemiousness, and common sense.

51. *Ya Sayyid! Ya Badawi! . . . July Ordinances!* Repeating a homely banality that originally had the character of a pious ejaculation, Hosny Allam invokes the name of Sayyid al-Badawi (d. 1275), a Muslim saint whose shrine in Tanta attracts crowds of a million or more during his annual *moulid.* Such an invocation ordinarily suggests astonishment tinged with some degree of moral sentiment and can thus be turned, as it is in Egypt and certainly is in this instance, to ironic effect. The July Ordinances of 1961 introduced socialism into Egypt, virtually creating a *coup d'état,* and may be compared in their rather different aims and effects with the July Ordinances promulgated in France in 1830.

52. *Camp de César.* See Note 41.

53. *Party business.* It should be understood that Mansour's friend Fawzi is a Communist, that the Communist Party has been outlawed by the regime, that Mansour has been forced by his brother to leave it, but has retained essential loyalty to it, and that his schizoid behaviour arises from this loyalty.

54. *loafing.* The original refers to Sarhan as an *habitué* of the *mastaba,* a low seat formerly found in front of shops or important houses, especially in villages, where men customarily gathered to gossip, talk politics, or discuss business. The *mastaba* is now often nostalgically identified with the supposed leisurely pace of traditional or country life, especially by urbanites, the *mastabas* of Cairo having been summarily removed as long ago as the eighteen-forties by order of that energetic Prince, Mohamed Aly, in the interests of improving the flow of traffic.

55. *board of directors . . . ASU Base Unit.* In accord with socialist measures that began to be implemented in 1961 and included the Charter (see Note 38), industrial and office workers were given twenty-five per cent of the shares in their firm's profits and seats on their firm's boards of directors. Scores of firms, including the entire banking and commercial network of the cotton industry, were nationalized, and the ASU (the Arab Socialist Union) became the sole instrument of popular democracy, with theoretical powers of direction at all levels. Sarhan represents the workers on the board of directors of the Alexandria Yarn Mills, but as an important and up-and-coming member of the ASU he is also, in effect, a member of the political body to which that board must answer. He has thus made a place for himself in what a capitalist would be tempted to define as four very different interest groups—government, stockholders, management, and labour—though it is obvious that Sarhan is the last person likely to be concerned by the multitudinous possibilities in such a situation for conflict of interest.

56. *conventional rhyming prose.* In Arabic, *saj'*, a prose mode that dates to earliest literary history among the Arabs and was consecrated by its association with the Koran, surviving all the way down to the present century, rhyme becoming in fact the primary rhetorical feature of consciously literary prose. The closest stylistic analogy to *saj'* in English is probably the short-lived euphuism identified with John Lyly (d. 1606) which may have been influenced by Arabic indirectly through North's translation of Guevara.

57. *the Auberge in Fayoum.* A formerly fashionable country resort south of Cairo.

58. *Blessed . . . of yours.* Sarhan does not say these words aloud, though the Egyptian, like the Spaniard or Latin-American with his *piropo*, (Blessed be the land where the tree grew from which they took the wood to make your cradle!), has a ready stock of flowery or provocative phrases to fire at passing girls, and can also improvise. A Cairo traffic policeman has been known to bring a thousand cars crashing to a halt in order to allow the unimpeded passage of a particular beauty, while declaiming a dozen lines or so made up on the spot to rhyme with the favoured girl's name.

59. *school-opening crisis.* For a family like Sarhan's finding the money for shoes and clothing alone would have meant a considerable sacrifice, in which he would naturally be expected to share.

60. *the wall.* Ali Bakir's sardonic humour here hinges on the fact that the direction of prayer, indicated in a mosque by the *qibla* niche in one wall, is also the direction in which one turns the face of the dead at burial.

61. *Ustaz.* Literally, 'professor', this word is used as the polite mode of addressing the presumably educated.

62. *the Revolution.* See notes 8, 38, and 55.

63. *Karmouz.* An inland slum district backing on the Mahmoudiya Canal.

64. *kissed my head.* Implying the desire for forgiveness and reconciliation, this typical gesture creates a tableau bearing an acerbic political symbolism that should not be lost.

65. *Or as darkness . . . the journeying.* Koran XXIV. 40–42 (The Sura of Light).

66. *The Beneficent . . . deny?* Koran LV. 1–13. See Notes 12 and 34.